LATIGO

Bounty hunter Latigo Rawlins was looking to start a whole new life with Emily Mercer, but Stillman Stadtlander has other plans for him. Latigo had given evidence that the landowner had arranged the deaths of rival Mexican ranchers, and now Stadtlander intends to see him pay — at the end of a rope. It doesn't matter to Emily that Latigo has notched up over a dozen killings himself. She is in love, and so she'll move heaven and earth to save the life of this man.

STEVE HAYES

LATIGO

Complete and Unabridged

LINFORD
Leicester

First published in Great Britain in 2013 by
Robert Hale Limited
London

First Linford Edition
published 2015
by arrangement with
Robert Hale Limited
London

A catalogue record for this book is available
from the British Library.

ISBN 978–1–4448–2357–8

Published by
F. A. Thorpe (Publishing)
Anstey, Leicestershire

Set by Words & Graphics Ltd.
Anstey, Leicestershire
Printed and bound in Great Britain by
T. J. International Ltd., Padstow, Cornwall

This book is printed on acid-free paper

For
Brian Taggert
A fine writer
An even better friend

1

They made a strange couple.

The man looked old enough to be the girl's father yet the loving way she held his hand as their buckboard pulled up to the train station in Las Cruces, New Mexico, suggested she was his girlfriend, not daughter.

She did not bear any resemblance to him, either. At sixteen, Emily Mercer was tall and slim with long, dark-brown hair and expressive brown eyes full of impudence mixed with a quiet gritty determination that warned everyone she would fight to get anything she wanted. She wasn't beautiful, but her fine-boned, oval face possessed such natural farm-fresh prettiness that men always found her worthy of a second look. It was the same with her clothes: though her autumn-colored coat, blouse, long skirt and button-top shoes were plain and simple, the regal way with which she carried herself made her attire seem as fashionable as any *haute couture* original from Paris.

The man holding the reins was her opposite in almost every way. Short and wiry, with curly hair yellow as corn, Latigo Rawlins was boyishly handsome with a splash of freckles and a smile that few women could resist. He wore an expensive western-styled black suit, string tie, hand-tooled boots and a pearl-gray Stetson that was so spotless it might have just come from its box. But his clothes couldn't hide his walk, talk or swaggering attitude: beneath all the finery still lived a barefoot, grubby-faced, rebellious boy from the sun-scorched dirt of the Texas Panhandle.

Except for his eyes. His eyes set him apart. They made him immediately menacing and lethal. Amber-colored, they were cold and merciless, and constantly on the move, wary of everything and everyone as if he expected death to strike at any moment — which is perhaps why he wore a gunbelt with two ivory-gripped, nickel-plated .44 six-guns tucked in worn-smooth black holsters that were tied down, gun-fighter fashion.

Now, as Latigo descended from the buckboard and tied the horse to the hitch-rail by the station entrance, he looked warily about him. Other than a disheveled drunk slumped against a wall, the area was empty. Latigo dug out a silver dollar and showed it to him. 'This is yours if you'll take the wagon back to Hal's Livery.'

The drunk grabbed the coin, mumbled his thanks and followed Latigo to the buckboard. Emily let Latigo help her down. Then, tucking her arm under his, she accompanied him to the small adobe stationhouse.

'He'll most likely spend it on whis-key,' Latigo said, 'but what the hell.'

'It's the thought that counts,' Emily said.

Inside, he bought two one-way tickets to Santa Rosa. 'Train's about ten minutes late,' he said, joining her on a waiting bench. 'Then we'll be on our way.'

'Sounds like you're looking forward to it — which is more than I am.'

'That's 'cause you don't know your pa like I do. He's no pushover, but he's a fair and reasonable man. He'll understand.'

She peered at him as if the summer heat had cooked his brains. 'Are we talking about the same Quint Longley? The drifter who for years came by my ranch to water his horse and have supper with me and my family, all the while knowing he was my father yet never intending to tell me?'

'He had his reasons. Good reasons. You know that, well as I do, Miss Emily.'

'Will you stop calling me Miss Emily,' she said crossly. 'Makes me feel like an old maid or a schoolteacher you just met at a church picnic. And I do believe our relationship has become more intimate than that.'

'I sure hope so,' Latigo said, 'else I

4

got you kicked out of school for nothin'.'

'*You* didn't get me kicked out,' Emily chided. 'I knew the rules when I sneaked out to meet you. I just hoped we weren't going to get caught.' She ruefully shook her head as if still not believing it. 'I swear those sisters are worse than watch dogs.'

'Yeah, and we gave them plenty to chew on.'

'My goodness, don't make it sound worse than it is. After all, Lat, we weren't doing anything sinful.'

'Still mighty embarrassin'.'

'But worth it,' she said, cuddling against him. 'Right? *Right*?' she repeated when he didn't reply.

Latigo nodded and grinned. 'C'mon,' he said, grasping her hand. 'Let's go outside. It can't be hotter than in here.'

★   ★   ★

After the train had come and gone, the drunk entered the stationhouse and went to the ticket-window. He still looked

5

disheveled but he no longer staggered as he walked, and when he spoke to the agent, he sounded sober.

'I want to send a wire to Mr Stillman J. Stadtlander,' he said.

The agent eyed him suspiciously. 'Costs money to send a wire, fella. You got any?'

The drunk put Latigo's silver dollar on the counter. 'That cover it?'

'Reckon. Depends on how many words.'

'Eight. 'They just boarded the train'.'

'That's only five words,' the agent said.

'The other three are for you,' the drunk said. He pulled a Colt .45 from under his filthy jacket, thumbed back the hammer and pressed the gun against the agent's forehead. 'Call. Me. Sir.'

'Y-Y-Yes, sir,' the panicked agent said. 'Anything you say, *sir*!'

2

When the train was about ten miles from Santa Rosa, a passenger seated behind Emily sneezed. The noise awakened Latigo. Rubbing his eyes, he looked around. Most of the other passengers were dozing. He gazed out the window. At first it appeared that nothing had changed outside — the flat monotonous sun-baked scrubland still stretched for endless miles in all directions, and the hazy purple-brown mountains still made up the distant horizon to the north. Yawning, he was about to doze off again, when he saw several riders approaching from the direction of town.

Too far away for him to identify, he watched intently as they came closer. He wasn't sure why but the sight of them made him uneasy. He continued to watch them ride purposefully toward the train; then, on impulse, decided to trust his instincts. He nudged Emily, who was dozing beside him. Waking, she blinked owlishly at him. 'Wha'?'

'I'm probably bein' antsy,' he said, 'but there're some riders approachin'.'

Emily looked out and saw the men rein up about fifty yards ahead of the speeding locomotive. Wheeling their horses around, they dug in their spurs and started galloping in the same direction as the train.

'They can't be looking for you, Lat. No one even knows we're on this train.'

'That's what I figured.'

'Then why are you worried? And don't say you aren't, 'cause I can hear it in your voice.'

'Not worried,' he corrected. 'Careful. In my business 'careful' keeps you alive.'

'What are you going to do?' she asked, as he stood up.

'Go sit over there.' He thumbed at an empty aisle seat a few rows ahead. 'Turns out for some reason I'm their target, pretend you don't know me.'

'But — '

'Emily,' he said, cutting her off, 'I promised I'd always look after you and you agreed to trust me — '

'I do trust you.'

'Then no arguments.' He winked at her reassuringly, turned and went to the empty seat. Few if any of the dozing passengers saw Latigo switch seats.

Emily nervously looked out the window. Outside, the half-dozen riders were now galloping alongside the train. By their clothing, she guessed they were cowhands — *heavily armed* cowhands, with tied-down six-guns and Winchesters tucked into the scabbards under their saddles.

One of the riders was close enough for her to see the brand on the rump of his horse. She recognized it immediately. Stadtlander's brand: the Double S.

Something cold and clammy dropped in her stomach.

So, she thought dismally, *it's started. Only one day out of school and already Stadtlander's gunmen have come to hang him!*

3

One by one, five of the men guided their galloping horses close to the last passenger car, grabbed something to cling to and swung aboard the train. The sixth rider reined up and remained behind to take care of the horses.

When all five men were on board they drew their guns and slowly made their way through the cars, checking each passenger as they did. It was obvious they were looking for someone — someone who by their grim, tight-lipped expressions and the tense way they held their guns was a threat to their lives.

They found him dozing in an aisle seat in the second car back from the locomotive: a small, dapper-looking man with blond curls and a freckled nose. Though armed with two holstered Colts, he looked harmless enough — until one gunman, a tall thin hollow-cheeked man named Sweets, prodded him with his gun.

Then he looked at the men gathered around him with wolfish-yellow eyes filled with such menace they stepped back, alarmed.

'Better have a good reason for wakin' me up,' Latigo said quietly.

Sweets wagged a gun in his face. 'Get up, *hombre*!'

'Please.'

'*Please?*' Sweets snorted, amused, while around him the other men laughed. 'You want me to say *please?*'

'Just common courtesy between pals.'

'Latigo,' Sweets said, teeth gritted, 'we was never pals. An' if'n I live to be a hundred, we never will be. To me you're nothin' but a mean-gutted, cold-hearted killer. An' when Mr Stadtlander strings you up, you runty-assed sonofabitch, I'll be the one whippin' the horse out from under you.'

Latigo Rawlins smiled — a frightening, thin-lipped smile that never reached his cold, yellow eyes. 'Sweets,' he said softly, 'you're not gonna live to be a hundred. Count on it.'

No one actually saw him move; not even Emily, who was seated across the aisle behind him and knew how fast he was. But she and the men *did* see the gun that almost magically appeared in his left hand — and they all heard the shot that followed.

All except Sweets, who staggered back and slumped lifelessly over the seats, blood coming from the bullet hole in his forehead.

On his feet now Latigo faced the other men. Despite the fact that they all had their guns out, he had the unmitigated gall to holster his .44 before saying, almost cheerfully: 'Hope he wasn't popular with you boys.'

None of them had the guts to reply — or move.

Latigo tipped his pearl gray Stetson politely at Emily. 'Sorry you had to see that, miss. But seems Mr Sweets, here' — he stared coldly at the corpse — 'was lackin' in manners. An' I surely *do* like a fella with manners.'

Stadtlander's men exchanged grim, uneasy looks. Then one of them, a squat, bearded, barrel-waisted man whose nickname was Amarillo, quickly pressed his gun against Emily's head.

'Unbuckle your irons,' he told Latigo, 'else this little flower of yourn never gets to reach Santa Rosa.' He paused, then added sarcastically, *'Por favor, señor.'*

Latigo shrugged indifferently. 'Go ahead, enjoy yourself,' he said. 'She don't mean burned beans to me.'

Amarillo grinned, showing brown broken teeth. 'Nice bluff. But this time Mr Stadtlander's holdin' all the aces.' He cocked the hammer back, adding, 'Her name's Emily Margaret Mercer. Her pa's Quint Longley, also known as Drifter. An' 'cause of you an' your moon-light visits, she's been booted out of St Marks.' He grinned even wider. 'How're them burned beans tastin' now, Lefty?'

Latigo did not move for a long,

13

chilling moment. But he paled and his jaw muscles clenched. Then slowly, eyes never leaving Amarillo, he unbuckled his gunbelt and handed it to the nearest man. Then he turned to Emily, who sat frozen in her seat with Amarillo's gun against her temple, and said, 'Like Pa was always sayin': 'No good deed goes unpunished'.'

Emily frowned, not understanding.

'The drunk I give the dollar to,' Latigo explained. 'He was one of theirs. Right?' he said to Amarillo.

'If you mean did he work for Mr Stadtlander — yeah. Been camped outside your little gal's school just waitin' for you to show up.'

Emily looked flabbergasted.

Latigo grunted, irked at himself. 'Carelessness,' he grumbled. 'First sign a fella's heart ain't his own.' Then to Amarillo, 'You got my guns an' I'm standin' up — so leather your iron an' let's put this business to bed.'

Amarillo nodded to one of the men, who reached up and pulled the emergency cord. The train came to an abrupt, brake-screeching, jolting stop. Passengers rocked in their seats, while the gunmen standing in the aisle staggered and grabbed anything within reach in order to keep their footing.

'Lat,' Emily began anxiously.

'It's all right,' he said calmly. 'Rope meant to stretch my neck ain't been braided yet.'

4

Drifter was standing on the tiny platform that encircled the top of the old watermill, repairing a broken vane, when he saw the rider approaching.

He stopped hammering and took a longer look. The rider was too far away to identify, especially blurred by the distant undulating heatwaves. Nor did he recognize the horse. But whoever it was, was pushing the horse hard, as if desperate to reach his destination — wherever that was — and for a moment Drifter felt uneasy. Admittedly, the ranch was within a few miles of Santa Rosa and seeing a rider or riders was not that unusual; but the ranch was also only a hard day's ride from Mexico and this rider, Drifter realized, could easily be border trash — riffraff on the run or just a renegade saddle bum looking for easy pickings.

Remembering he was unarmed, Drifter decided not to take any chances. Climbing down, he hurried to the single-level, log-walled house that had been his home since Emily had left for school. When he reappeared he had buckled on his gunbelt and was holding a .45-.70 caliber Winchester '86. Hanging around his neck were a pair of old US Army field glasses. Leaning the rifle against the porch post, he focused the glasses on the fast-approaching rider. He twisted the lenses around until suddenly the rider appeared clearly in his vision.

He was so surprised by who it was that he had to take a second look to make sure he wasn't imagining things. He wasn't.

'*Emily*,' he breathed, not realizing he'd thought aloud. 'What the hell . . . ?'

* * *

Bringing the exhausted, lathered horse to a sliding stop, Emily slid from the saddle before Drifter could help her down. She was caked with sweat. Her clothes were grimy with trail dust and her normally neat hair was windblown and matted about her face. But she didn't seem to notice or care. Hugging him, she buried her face in his chest and began sobbing.

'What is it?' he said, stroking her head. 'What's wrong?'

She blurted something he couldn't understand.

'Emily . . . honey, I can't hear you . . . What's happened? What're you doin' here?'

He could feel her trying to fight back her tears. Hoping to soothe her, he continued to hold her and to stroke her head. After a little, she calmed down enough to raise her head and look at him, eyes still flooded with tears.

'It's L-Latigo,' she finally managed to say.

Drifter frowned, surprised to hear the gun-fighter's name mentioned by his daughter. 'What about him?'

'Stadtlander's going to hang him,' she

said, sniffing back her tears.

'First, they got to find him.'

'They already found him. Stadtlander's men — they took him from the train this morning.'

'Train? What train?' Before she could answer, he added, 'Emily, I don't know what you're talkin' about. And 'fore we go any further, I reckon we'd better go inside . . . get you somethin' cool to drink . . . an' then, maybe, we can sit down an' you can tell me what this is all about.'

'No, no, there isn't time, Daddy. We have to ride over there now, find a way to stop them somehow — '

'Ride over where — to the Double S?'

'Yes, yes. Don't you see?' she said, hammering her fists on his chest. 'Stadtlander's been trying to get his hands on Latigo ever since he signed that lawyer's letter proving Stadtlander paid him to kill those Mexican ranchers — '

'I know, sweetheart, I was there,

remember? But what I can't figure out is how you're involved, an' why you're standin' here 'stead of bein' in school, like you should be.'

Emily stepped back and stood tall, took a deep breath, as if preparing herself for his eventual outburst, then said, 'Father, I'm not at St Marks anymore. I've been expelled.'

Drifter's dark eyebrows arched with surprise. Suddenly he had a hundred questions to ask. But he controlled himself and putting an arm about her shoulders, said quietly, 'Let's go inside, honey. Reckon you got some healthy explainin' to do.'

Reluctantly, she nodded and let him lead her into the house.

5

Indoors, at her father's insistence, she washed her face, pinned her hair back and changed into a clean shirt, jeans and boots and then, only then, would he listen to her story. They sat at the old plank supper table made twenty years ago by Frank Mercer — the man whom, until recently, she had believed was her father — each drinking a glass of buttermilk kept cool in a pan of water in the pantry. In fits and starts, she explained how, a few months ago, Latigo Rawlins had showed up at St Marks. Claiming to be her uncle, he asked the mother superior if he could talk to his niece. Charmed by the little Texan's smile and charming manners, Mother Clarissa had not only agreed but had allowed them to sit and talk in the shady schoolyard and had even asked one of the sisters to bring them lemonade.

'What did Lefty want?' Drifter said, interrupting Emily.

'I just told you — to talk to me.'

''Bout what?'

Emily hesitated. She could tell by her father's tone of voice that he was already displeased, and knew that she had to be very careful how she explained what had happened, or he would close his mind on the matter before she could convince him that she and Latigo were in love.

'Nothing particular,' she said at last. 'He happened to be in Las Cruces and thought he'd see how I was doing. That's all.'

'Man's lyin' through his teeth,' Drifter said.

'Daddy — !'

'He's wanted for five murders, for Chris'sake. Any lawman catches him this side of the border he ends up dancin' from a rope. Why would Latigo — who's 'bout as warm-hearted and carin' as a rattler — risk his life to see you?'

'He's likes me,' Emily said. 'And I like him. Don't look like that,' she added, seeing his scowl. 'You knew that when I went off to school.'

He did but he didn't want to remember it. 'Speakin' of school, missy, how come you got expelled? 'Cordin' to your last letter, you were doin' fine with your studies. Were you tellin' me tall tales?'

' 'Course not. You know I'm no liar.'

'Thought I did.'

'Well, I'm not.' She paused, trying to find a placating way of saying what she had to say. But there was no placating way, and realizing this and that every minute they talked was another minute they were not rescuing Latigo, she looked her father directly in the eyes and said, 'I was expelled because I broke one of the cardinal rules. And before you ask me which one, it's about not leaving the school grounds for any reason without permission from Mother Clarissa or one of the sisters.'

Drifter looked surprised. 'What did you leave for? Wait a minute,' he said

before she could answer. 'You sayin'
you snuck out to see Latigo?'

'Yes.'

'Judas.'

'Don't make it sound like I robbed a
bank or something.'

'That might be the lesser of two
evils,' Drifter muttered grimly. 'Where'd
you go?'

'Nowhere. Lat was waiting for me
outside the gate and we walked a little
ways and found a place to sit and, well,
we just sat there and talked.'

'An' that's where you were when they
caught you — the sisters, I mean?'

'Uh-huh. Sister Velasquez, to be exact.'

Drifter mulled her story over for a
few moments, sensing something important was missing, and then said: 'What
time was this?'

'Late,' she said vaguely.

'Night, you mean?' When she nodded,
he said, 'What are nuns doin' out walkin'
around at night for?'

Realizing she could stall no longer,
Emily sighed and said, 'It was almost

morning by then. You know how time flies when you're talking,' she added quickly. 'Heavens, I didn't mean to stay out all night, but — '

'If talkin' was all you were doin',' he said suspiciously.

'What do you *think* we were doing?'

'I don't want to think. I want you to tell me. Now.'

'All right,' she blurted, 'I will. We were kissing. We were kissing and hugging when Sister Velasquez caught us and reported us to Mother Clarissa. So there! Now you know everything. Go on,' she added quickly, 'yell at me. Curse me if you want. Call me dirty names. I don't care. I love Latigo and he loves me. And we're going to get married and no one in the world is going to stop us — not even you!'

'I won't have to,' Drifter said grimly. 'Stadtlander an' a rope will take care of that for me.'

Emily glared at him, eyes filling with tears. 'That's a hateful, wicked thing to say! And I hate you for saying it!'

Jumping up, she stormed into her bedroom.

Drifter looked after her and sighed away his frustration. 'Right 'bout now,' he said softly, 'I hate myself for sayin' it too.'

After a few minutes Emily appeared in the doorway of her bedroom. Her eyes were raw from crying and, as she stood there looking at Drifter, she angrily twisted a handkerchief around her fingers.

'Father, are you going to help me try to save Latigo or not?'

He finished rolling a smoke then licked the paper, sealing it, and stuck it between his lips. Flaring a match on his jeans, he inhaled and spat out a thin stream of smoke before saying, 'I'll not help a gunman so he can marry my daughter — 'specially when she's only sixteen.'

'I'm almost seventeen.'

'Sixteen, seventeen — a hundred an' seventeen — answer's the same.'

Emily shook her head in disgust.

'Shame on you, Father. Shame on you for running out on a friend who's helped you in the past.'

Drifter laughed mirthlessly. 'First off, Daughter mine, I've known Latigo a hell of a lot longer than you and believe me, he's got no friends but himself. An' secondly, if there's any shame to be spread around, I reckon it falls on you for defendin' a bounty-hunter an' a shootist who's gunned down more'n a dozen men, some of 'em for no reason other than they stepped on his ego.'

'I'm not defending Latigo,' Emily said sharply. 'I think it's terrible what he's done. And I've told him so, many times. But God tells us to forgive others their sins and that's what I've tried to do. Besides, plenty of others have killed — including you — and that doesn't stop me from loving you, so why shouldn't I love him as well?'

'If you're comparin' me to Latigo Rawlins,' Drifter said angrily, 'then I reckon there's no reason for me to stay here, fixin' this place up so you'll have a home to come back to after finishin' school — which now it 'pears you won't. An' there's plenty of shame in that.' Rising, he walked out the door before she could say anything.

The thought of losing her father, as well as Latigo, momentarily overwhelmed Emily. She sank down on a chair, covered her face with her hands and wondered how a world that only yesterday had seemed so perfect, could now turn against her.

But she was no weak-kneed sister. Neither did she enjoy feeling sorry for herself. So, angrily pulling herself together, she marched outside and looked around for her father. He was entering the barn. She called to him, stopping him in the doorway, and ran across the open area that separated the house from the barn and corrals, and confronted him.

'I'm sorry,' she said. 'I had no right to say what I did. You're a far better, more decent man than Latigo. I know that. Everyone in Santa Rosa knows that. I was just angry at you and — and, well, you know how I get when I'm — oh, please forgive me, Daddy. I'm really ashamed of myself.'

Drifter smiled — a warm smile that crinkled his rugged, weathered face. 'Apology accepted,' he said. He put his arms around her and pulled her close. 'Only reason I came down hard on you, Daughter mine, is 'cause I love you an' want you to be happy. You know that, don't you?'

' 'Course.'

'You talk about bein' ashamed: well, I'm ashamed of myself for not bein' around to protect you all those years you were growin' up. But I'm here now. I'm here an' I intend to make up for it by lookin' out for you . . . makin' sure you're happy an' that nothin' bad happens to you. Understand?'

Emily nodded. 'But you must understand something too, Daddy. When it comes to loving Lat, *I* can't help myself — anymore than you or *Momma* could. I honestly can't. I know it sounds crazy. I even keep telling myself I'm crazy. But that doesn't stop me from loving him. Oh, I know who he is, *what* he is, and what folks will think of me for even considering marrying him — and that includes me sometimes. I mean I was raised by the Good Book rules, taught never to raise my hand in anger. Yet despite that, I can love a man like Latigo. Good heavens, Daddy, you think you're upset about what's happened, well, Momma and Pa Mercer would have been horrified, more than horrified, had they ever found out.' She paused, visualizing just how angry and hurt and ashamed they would have been, and then said, 'May I ask you something, something personal that you probably won't answer?'

'How did I feel when I realized I loved your momma?'

Emily nodded. 'Knowing you, even little as I do, it must've made you feel guilty knowing she was married — and worse, to a good man, a man you considered your friend, a man who had children to raise.'

Drifter said, 'It chewed at me back then and now, almost eighteen years later, it's still chewin' at me. Reckon it always will.'

'Momma too, I imagine — while she was alive.'

'Told me it was like walkin' around with a knife stuck in her.'

'Yet it didn't stop you . . . either of you . . . from . . . making a baby.'

Drifter was silent as he mulled over his answer. Then he stepped back, cupped her face between his hands and studied her, his expression sad but grateful as he said gently, 'No, it didn't. That's the damnation of love. Once it gets hold of you, seems like a madness takes over an' you find yourself ignoring what's right or wrong, or decent, an' just blindly do what it tells you to. An' you know what?' he added. 'Now I'm damn' glad I did. I mean, sinful as what your ma an' me done, havin' you be the result of our union has made all the pain and guilt worthwhile — more'n worthwhile.'

Emily didn't know what to say. She felt great warmth welling up inside her. Tears rushing to her eyes, she pressing against him and hugged him like it was the last time she'd ever see him.

6

It was late afternoon but still sweltering hot inside the barn and Latigo felt rivulets of sweat running down his back under his shirt.

The heat was also causing problems for the ranch-hand guarding him. Seated on some loose hay he'd spread on the floor a few hours earlier when he'd relieved the prior guard, he was fighting not to fall asleep. He sat slumped against the side of an empty stall, constantly nodding off then waking up with a grunt, blinking like a startled owl as he stared about him, for an instant wondering where he was and how long he'd been asleep. Then as he recognized his surroundings and reality returned, he relaxed and looked at his prisoner. Each time the sight of Latigo securely roped to one of the large center-posts supporting the barn roof brought a sigh of relief from the young man. He'd then roll a smoke or walk outside, rifle in hand, and splash water on his face from the trough, returning moments later to sit in the same place and lean back against the stall — only to yawn and gradually drift off to sleep again.

Watching him through lidded eyes, Latigo appeared to be half-asleep himself. But behind the post, unseen by the ranch-hand, he was desperately trying to untie the knots binding his wrists. It seemed hopeless. The knots refused to co-operate. But Latigo, never one to admit defeat, continued tugging at them anyway.

Time's running out, he thought grimly. If he didn't get loose soon, a new hand would arrive to guard him and then, four hours later, another, and so on through the night. Then, at dawn, the ranch would come alive as all the other ranch-hands, many of them gunmen like he'd been when he'd worked for Stadtlander, went about their work-day; some of them, like Stadtlander's son, Slade, and maybe his cronies, the Iverson brothers, would be checking on him from time to time, making escape almost impossible.

Damn his feelings for Emily, he thought. *Damn her, too!* If she hadn't entered his life he'd still be holed up somewhere in Chihuahua, safe from Stadtlander's men and enjoying life with nothing more on his mind than bedding some fiery, dark-eyed whore — instead of being only a 'train arrival' away from a noose!

Because earlier that afternoon, after the men had enjoyed themselves punching him around, he'd heard them yammering about how they couldn't hang him until the boss arrived on tomorrow morning's train. And though that was still many hours off, the little Texan didn't have to think too hard to visualize Stadtlander's gloating smirk as he watched a rope being tossed over the branches of the oak trees shading the west wall of the big ranch-house.

Goddamn him anyway, Latigo thought

35

bitterly. *Him an' his goddamn money an' his goddamn lawyers an' his goddamn ability to somehow always dodge punishment for the crimes he paid to have committed* —

Loud, raucous laughter coming from the bunkhouse interrupted his thoughts. He glanced at the young hand snoring faintly a few feet away. Now, he told his fingers. *Do it now!*

But the knots held firm, forcing Latigo Rawlins to realize that he really might hang tomorrow morning. He really and truly might!

7

The two of them rode across the hot, open scrubland at a steady, mile-consuming lope. Neither spoke. Both had their reasons. The man, because he was still angry at himself for agreeing to do something he not only didn't want to do but knew eventually, if not sooner, would cause his daughter nothing but grief; the girl, because she was desperately trying to convince herself that they were not already too late to save the man she loved from hanging.

And even if they weren't too late, she reasoned, what then? There were just two of them against at least forty experienced gunmen, all willing to obey every order issued by their boss, Stillman J. Stadtlander, a rich and powerful cattleman known for his ruthless, vengeful nature. And though she had faith in her father, believing him capable of conquering any problem, deep down she sensed that this time she had asked too much of him.

Ahead, the trail forked in opposite directions. One trail led to Santa Rosa, the other to Stadtlander's ranch, the Double S. To her surprise, and dismay, her father headed toward town.

'W-What're you doing?' she demanded, reining up. 'You're going the wrong way.'

Drifter pulled up his horse and looked back at her. 'Not if you want to save Latigo.'

'I don't understand,' Emily said. 'Why would Stadtlander hang Lat in Santa Rosa?'

'He wouldn't.'

'Then — ?'

'Accordin' to Lars Gustavson, Stadtlander's in Deming with his lawyers, preparin' to file another appeal so he can stall off goin' to trial end of this month.'

For a moment she didn't see the connection. Then it hit her and her sunburned face lit up with a smile. 'Oh,

I get it — so long as he's in Deming, his men won't hang Lat.'

'That's what I'm countin' on. An' supposedly, he ain't due back till mornin'.'

'I hate you,' she said, not meaning it. 'You knew Lat was safe all along but you let me rant and rave and cry and in general make a silly fool of myself without telling me.'

'Somethin' like that.'

'Oh Daddy, how could you?' Then before he could reply, 'But I still don't understand why we're going into town. I mean, surely Stadtlander's men are holding Lat out at the ranch, not in jail. And anyway, from what Lat told me, the new sheriff only got elected because he was bankrolled by Stadtlander. Just like Lonnie Forbes was before him.'

'True. But I need to send a wire. An' the closest telegraph office is — '

' — in Santa Rosa,' she finished for him.

'Somethin' like that.' Drifter gently tapped the sorrel's flanks with his spurs, then swore and jerked his foot aside as Wilson, irascible as ever, tried to bite him before grudgingly breaking into a trot.

Emily giggled, despite her mood, and with a flick of the reins sent the magnificent, blue roan stallion, El Diablo, cantering after them.

★ ★ ★

Once they reached Santa Rosa, a small but prosperous town that was located alongside the railroad roughly halfway between El Paso and Deming, Emily stopped to return the horse she'd borrowed from Gustafson's Livery while her father rode on to the telegraph office on Front Street. There, he had the operator wire the US Marshal's office in El Paso:

DEPUTY US MARSHAL MACAHAN URGENTLY NEEDED IN SANTA ROSA TO PREVENT POTENTIAL LYNCHING STOP STADTLANDER INVOLVED STOP SHERIFF USELESS STOP IF

CANT GET HERE BY TOMORROW
LATEST REPLY IMMEDIATELY STOP
QUINT LONGLEY

After the operator had sent the wire
he looked nervously at Drifter and
asked: 'Who's the unlucky party?'

'You, if you breathe one word of this,'
Drifter warned. 'An' that means to
anybody! Got it?'

'Got it,' the operator said, adding, 'If
there's an answer, mister, where can I
find you?'

'Gustafson's or the sheriff's office.
An' make sure you don't stop for a beer
on the way.' He walked out, leaving the
telegraph operator shaking his head.

★   ★   ★

When Drifter entered the livery stable
he found Emily playing chess with the
old, gray-bearded owner, Lars Gustafson,
who was hobbled by arthritis.

'Thought you were a checkers man?'
Drifter said.

41

'Was,' Gustafson said. 'Now Lonnie's dead I learn to play chess.'

'I'm teaching him,' Emily said. 'In payment for letting me borrow his horse this morning.'

'Can't pay bills with chess lessons,' Drifter said, digging out money. 'How much, Lars?'

'You're wasting your time,' Emily said. 'I already tried to pay — '

Gustafson raised a leathery hand, silencing her. Then, spitting snuff juice into a bucket by his feet, he looked up from the board at Drifter. 'Her money's no good here. Neither's yourn.'

'Why's that?'

'Apparently Pa Mercer loaned Mr Gustafson money when he needed it,' Emily explained.

'Twice,' the white-haired Swede said. 'Back in '65, when my Greta an' me, we come here from old country and I need a stake to open blacksmith shop, then in '78, when the Apache uprisin' chased all my business away. Greta an' me, we are all set to pack up'n leave,

42

but your pa — I mean Pa Mercer,' he corrected himself — 'paid my bills till, little by little, new folks started settlin' here an' I do OK again.'

'Sounds like Frank,' Drifter said. 'Always willing to help someone in need.' He teasingly ruffled Emily's hair. 'He even managed to work his magic with you.'

'Thanks for the seal of approval,' she said pithily. Then as Gustafson started to move his knight, 'No, no, no, a knight's worth much more than a pawn. Take my pawn with your pawn — see, like this.' She demonstrated.

Gustafson spat again and shook his head. 'I never learn this game, I think. Not enough brains.' Then to Drifter, 'I heard 'bout Latigo. Damn fool. Why'd he leave Mexico to come up here an' risk a rope party?'

'Goin' to ask him that very same question next time I see him,' Drifter said. He turned to Emily. 'I'll be at the sheriff's office 'case you need me.'

'I'll go with you,' she said, rising.

'Now, you practice,' she added to Gustafson. 'I expect you to beat me next time we play.'

The old Swede grinned, revealing more gum than teeth. 'I ain't plannin' on livin' that long, Miss Emily. Want me to grain the horses?' he asked Drifter.

'Yeah. If things don't turn out the way I'm hopin', they're goin' to need all the stamina they can get.'

8

When Drifter and Emily entered the sheriff's office, they found the lawman sitting at his desk, feet up, playing Shelvin' Rock on his fiddle. He kept on playing, beaming at them as if he expected them to start dancing; then, when they didn't, he frowned, sighed, grudgingly lowered his feet and stared at them over his fiddle.

'Yes, folks?' he said, his accent indicating he was a transplanted easterner. 'How may my office serve you today?'

Drifter came straight to the point. 'How d'you feel 'bout lynchin'?'

Some of the façade of joviality disappeared from Sheriff Wirter's watery blue eyes. In his early fifties, he was built like a rain barrel with a halo of white hair around a large bald spot, giving him the appearance of an ageing cherub. 'Why I'm against it, of course — just like any officer of the law would be. Why do you ask, sir?'

'Then I can count on your help should one happen?'

'Definitely. That's why the good citizens of Santa Rosa elected me — they knew they could trust me to uphold the law.' He added nervously, 'There's not going to be a lynching, is there?'

'Depends.'

'On what?'

'How soon your boss gets back from Deming.'

'Mayor Curtis has gone to Deming? But I just saw him earlier — '

'Not the mayor. The man who bought you that tin star: Stillman J. Stadtlander.'

The sheriff froze, momentarily panicked, and then forced himself to laugh. 'You joke, of course, sir.'

Emily said, 'Do we look like we're joking?'

'Well, n-no, miss ... but Mr Stadtlander, my Lord he would never lynch anyone. I mean . . . you must be mistaken.'

'But if I ain't,' Drifter said, 'an' he tries to string up this fella I know, you'd stop him, right?'

The sheriff swallowed, hard. 'Naturally. As a former constable — '

'Part-time constable — '

' — in Deming — '

'Who was fired for takin' bribes.'

The sheriff paled, gulped, then blustered, 'That is a complete and utter lie. All charges agin me were dropped and — '

'Not dropped,' Drifter said relentlessly, 'plea-bargained out by one of Stadtlander's lawyers so you could pay a fine 'stead of goin' to jail. That is the proper legal term, ain't it,' he added to Emily, 'for side-steppin' the law?'

'It is indeed,' she said.

The sheriff, in an effort to salvage what was left of his pride, said, 'This man you claim might be lynched — would that be the outlaw Latigo Rawlins?'

'Well, well,' Drifter said. 'Seems you ain't as . . . as . . . ' He turned to Emily. 'What's that word I'm lookin' for?'

'Uninformed.'

'Uninformed as you led us to believe.' His tone hardened. 'Now, everyone knows Stadtlander's got you in his pocket, but whether you like it or not you're still a lawman who took an oath to uphold the law an' defend folks' rights — ' He stopped as the door swung open and the telegraph operator hurried in.

Seeing Drifter, he handed him a wire. 'Here's your answer, mister.'

Drifter read the wire. He smiled, greatly relieved. Digging out a coin, he flipped it to the operator who hurried out. He then turned back to Wirter. 'Reckon you can get on with your fiddlin' now, Sheriff. C'mon, Emily.' He stepped to the door, opened it for her and followed her out.

Outside on the sun-yellowed sidewalk Emily took two steps and then stopped. 'All right, Father, what's going on?'

Drifter waved the wire at her. 'Help's on the way.'

Puzzled, Emily took the wire and read it; then, as if she didn't believe what she'd read, read it again, this time aloud: 'WILL BE ON EVENING TRAIN STOP MEET ME AT STATION STOP DEPUTY US MARSHAL MACAHAN. Oh my goodness,' she exclaimed, handing back the wire. 'That's wonderful news!'

'Best lawman west of St Louis.'

'Yes, and we know he's not afraid to stand up to Mr Stadtlander — '

'Or turn a blind eye to a lynchin'.'

'I feel better already,' Emily said. 'Only thing I don't understand is if you were expecting Marshal Macahan, why'd you bother riling up Sheriff Wirter?'

'I wanted to find out how much he knew 'bout Latigo's capture an' where he stood on it, 'case there's a showdown.'

'He's Stadtlander's puppet: what did you expect?'

'Never can tell 'bout puppets, Emily. Sometimes they let someone pull the strings till they get what they want an' then cut ties with them. I've seen it happen afore.'

'You're right,' she said, thinking about Lonnie Forbes, the former sheriff of Santa Rosa who had turned in his star so he could help her recover her stolen horses, only to be killed by Comancheros. 'But I doubt that will be the case with our fiddling sheriff. He's more likely to wire Mr Stadtlander and report everything you said.'

'I'm countin' on it.'

'I don't follow you.'

Folding the wire and tucking it in his shirt pocket, Drifter said, 'I want the sonofabitch to be here when Macahan takes Latigo into custody.'

'Why?'

'So's I can watch the old bastard eat crow. With the trial hangin' over him, he can't afford another run-in with the law — 'specially Federal law. He'll just have to stand by, grindin' his teeth, while we all ride away.'

'You're an evil man, Mr Longley,' Emily said, as Drifter grinned at the thought. 'But I must admit, the thought pleases me, too.'

''Course,' Drifter said, 'bringin' Macahan in could cause a problem.'

'Such as? Oh my God,' she exclaimed, remembering. 'You said 'when Macahan takes Latigo into custody'.'

'Uh-huh.'

Emily made a face. 'Lat's not going to be happy about that.'

'Would he be happier to have his neck stretched?'

'You're right,' she said, not sounding convinced. 'We must be sure to remind him of that alternative when he throws a fit.'

9

It had spoken volumes about the growing prosperity of Santa Rosa when the Southern Pacific had built a spur that connected the town to the recently-completed Sunset Route — the main line stretching from New Orleans to California — and agreed to stop there if any passenger wished to get off.

That evening only one passenger got off and he was from El Paso. It was already dark but the lights of the station-house showed a tall, wide-shouldered, dark-haired man in his mid-twenties, with a drooping gun-fighter mustache, wearing a black, flat-brimmed hat, black suit and string tie, and an ebony-grip Colt .45 holstered on his right hip. He had no carpetbag, but over his left shoulder hung saddle-bags and a rolled-up slicker.

' 'Evenin', Ezra,' Drifter said, shaking

hands with the lawman. 'You remember my daughter, Emily, I expect?'

'I do indeed.' Deputy US Marshal Macahan politely tipped his hat. 'Ma'am.'

'Good evening, Marshal.' Emily smiled and chided herself for not remembering how ruggedly attractive Macahan was — or *how young* to have already earned such a glowing reputation. 'It's wonderful to see you again.'

Macahan gave a tight-lipped smile that vanished almost immediately; then, all business, said to Drifter, 'I'll need a horse. Wasn't room for mine on the train on such short notice.'

'No problem,' Drifter said. 'I already spoke to Lars Gustafson. Said when we stop by in the mornin', he'll saddle one up for you.'

'Morning?' Macahan frowned. 'What about Stadtlander an' this 'urgent' lynchin' you wired me 'bout?'

'Mr Stadtlander's in Deming on business,' Emily explained. 'He can't get here till tomorrow morning earliest — '

'What 'bout his men? Why do they

need to wait for him to lynch someone?'

'In most cases I'm sure they wouldn't,' Emily said, 'but since this is such a personal issue with Mr Stadtlander, I — my father and I feel they won't dare hang Lat till he arrives.'

'Lat?'

'Latigo Rawlins.'

Macahan's dark eyebrows arched angrily. '*That's* what this is all about — a cold-blooded bounty hunter gettin' his neck stretched by the murderin' bastard who hired him? Jesus-on-a-cross, Quint, why the hell didn't you say so 'fore you dragged me over here?'

Drifter shrugged. 'Reckon you just answered that question yourself.'

'Don't blame my father,' Emily said quickly. 'If it had been strictly up to him he probably wouldn't have wired you. I'm the one he did it for.'

'You?'

'Yes. I'm very fond of Latigo.'

Macahan looked disbelievingly at Drifter, who shrugged, indicating he was as flabbergasted as the lawman.

'Therefore,' Emily continued, 'I'm the one you should be angry at — if you should be angry at all, which, quite frankly, Marshal, I don't think you should.'

'You don't, huh?'

'No. After all, you are the law. And as such, it's your sworn duty to make sure everyone — even a bounty hunter — is treated fairly, or at the very least, according to the law, and not 'get their neck stretched', as you so aptly put it, on the say-so of a man as ruthless and vindictive as Mr Stadtlander!'

Deputy US Marshal Macahan shot Drifter an angry look, as if to say he was holding him responsible for Emily's tongue-lashing; then, with gritted restraint, he said to Emily, 'Don't worry 'bout me doin' my sworn duty, Miss Mercer. Sun ain't yet dawned on a day when I haven't followed the law down to the last letter.'

'Then Latigo has nothing to worry about,' she said.

'Nothing 'cept the rope I'm goin' to hang him with,' Macahan said tersely — 'legally of course.' He turned to Drifter.

'I'll meet you at Gustafson's at sunup.'

'I'll be there.'

'So will I,' put in Emily.

Macahan ignored her. 'If that's it,' he said to Drifter, 'reckon I'll mosey on over to the hotel — less'n of course you have some *other* 'urgent' matters that require my service?'

'Nope. Here . . . ' Drifter dug out a hotel key and handed it to the lawman. 'Room's already paid for.'

'I'll make sure you get your money back,' Macahan said. 'Marshal's office pays for my expenses. That way' — he included Emily — 'no one can accuse me of takin' bribes.' He walked off.

'Well,' Drifter said, 'that went well.'

'And to think,' Emily said scathingly, 'I once really liked that man.'

They started across the street into town.

'Tact,' Drifter said.

'What?'

'Tact.'

'What about it?'

'Reckon it's somethin' the sisters forgot to teach you at St Marks.'

10

Rather than ride all the way to the ranch and then back again before sunup, Drifter and Emily accepted the Gustafsons' offer to spend the night in their adobe house behind the livery stable. There was only one extra bedroom which naturally Emily took, while Drifter was given the old flower-patterned sofa in the parlor. 'It is much comfortable,' Greta Gustafson assured him during supper. 'Is that not true, my husband?'

'Yes, my pigeon,' the old Swede replied. He rolled his eyes at Drifter, who managed not to grin. 'Much comfortable. Though I 'spect it might be a tad short for them long legs of yours.'

'I was thinkin' the same thing,' Drifter said. 'Maybe I'd be better off in the stable.'

'Such men talk,' Greta said disapprovingly. She was a tiny, perky little white-haired woman who moved like a sparrow. 'Never a choice like this would be made in the old country. Only out here, where the sunsets die, does a man prefer straw to a civilized sofa.'

After supper, while Emily was helping Greta to wash the dishes, Drifter offered to buy Lars a drink at the cantina.

'My Lars, he does not imbibe,' Greta said before he could answer. 'Except for a sip of the eggnog on festive occasions. Is that not right, my husband?'

'Never a truer word was spoke,' Lars said. 'But,' he added quickly to Drifter, 'a game of checkers, now that'd be right welcome.'

'You're on,' Drifter said. He handed the old hostler his walking stick and helped him hobble out before the women could stop them.

Emily finished drying the last dish and then thought wistfully for a moment before saying: 'Mrs Gustafson, would you mind if I ask you something personal?'

'You go right ahead, my dear. It is to answer questions of the young that one grows old.'

'Did people ever tell you not to marry Mr Gustafson?'

'What means people?'

'You know, like your folks or grandparents — relatives, friends — anyone who was close to you?'

'Ahh,' Greta said. She gave a crinkly smile and cocked her head, birdlike. 'You have boy you found who is not approved of by your father?'

'Well, he's not exactly a boy,' Emily said, 'but, yes, my father doesn't approve of him. In fact he's dead set against me even liking him.'

'Was same with me once,' Greta admitted. She paused to dry her tiny wrinkled hands on a dish cloth, mind traveling back into the past, which she seemed to find wryly amusing. 'My Poppa, he was *borgmastare* of our little town my family we live in. He has much grand ideas for me, his only one daughter, and he not so' — she

59

searched a moment for the right word — 'impressed by this man I love, Lars.'

'So, what did you do? I mean did you elope?'

Greta frowned. 'I not know this word, elope.'

'You know — ran off with and got married?'

'Ahh, yes, yes, this we did.' Greta giggled like a child with a secret. 'We elope very much.'

'Oh, what fun!'

'Yes, yes, fun indeed.'

'So what happened — after you got married, I mean?'

'What happened is we not ever go home, we come here,' Greta said simply.

''Mean you never saw your folks or family again?'

'Not for much years, my dear. Then, when my Lars, he is successful blacksmith, we write letter of invite to my parents. But by then,' Greta said darkly, 'they are so old and once they get here they not live long.'

'Oh my goodness,' Emily said, crushed.

'That is so sad, Mrs Gustafson.'

'Yes,' Greta agreed. 'Much sad. But,' she added cheerfully, 'my Lars, he bury them here in cemetery so this way I get to talk to them many times as I want.'

11

In the livery stable, Drifter and Lars sat hunched over the old, snuff-stained checker board, their every move illuminated by a nearby hurricane lamp that cast their elongated shadows on the rear wall.

'I see you ain't lost your touch,' Drifter grumbled as Lars jumped two of his men and motioned for him to 'king' his checker. 'I was hopin' maybe playin' chess had taken the edge off your game.'

The old Swede glanced around to make sure they were alone, then took a swig of jug-whiskey before confiding, 'Do not be tellin' Miss Emily what I'm sayin', but this chess game it ain't for me. Too much thinkin' makes my brains ache — '

He broke off as gunshots were fired outside. Men started hollering. More shots followed. Then, more shouting. And finally silence.

Drifter, head cocked in the direction of the shooting, said: 'Am I loco, or was one of them voices a gal's?'

'Sure sounded that way,' Lars said. With the help of his stick, he struggled to his feet and followed Drifter to the big double-doors. Both cautiously poked their heads out and looked up and down the street.

'By God,' Drifter breathed. 'Will you look at that!'

A short distance on along Main Street, opposite Rosario's Cantina, stood a tall, lean but sturdy woman wearing a campaign hat, a long duster over a sun-faded blue denim shirt and soiled Levi's tucked into knee-high shit kickers. Her back was turned to Drifter so he could not see her face. But he could see she was holding a still-smoking Colt .44 and looking down at the rough-looking, bearded gunman who lay dying at her feet.

Drifter heard the man cursing at the

woman. Unfazed, she hunkered down beside him and gently wadded his hat under his head like a pillow. 'You don't have long,' she told him. 'If I was you, Henry, I'd be makin' peace with my Maker, not cussin' me.'

'Damn you to hell,' the gunman said. They were his last words. His head slumped and the woman sighed, troubled, and stood up.

Behind her Drifter saw townspeople emerging from the various stores, hotels, restaurants and cantinas lining both sides of Main Street. One of them was Macahan. Unhurried, the tall, big-shouldered young Deputy US Marshal idly picked at his teeth with a toothpick as he headed for the woman.

'Be right back,' Drifter told Lars. Giving the old Swede no time to argue, he strode off down the street.

By the time he reached her, she was explaining what had happened to Macahan. Drifter eased his way through the crowd that had gathered around them. On reaching the woman's side, he heard her say: ' . . . soon as he started shooting I had no choice but to shoot back.' She paused and shook her head. 'Damnedest thing, Ezra . . . no matter how many times I warn these fellas, they just don't believe me — till it's too late.'

'It's the times,' Macahan said laconically. 'Out here, way most men figure, a woman's only good for cookin', whorin' an' havin' babies. Try to tell them anythin' different an' like Fennedy here, they just can't circle their brains around it.'

'Reckon not,' Liberty said. Holstering her Colt, she looked at the corpse, genuinely regretting that she'd had to kill him. 'Marshal Thompson warned me it'd be like this, you know, when he swore me in. Said if I wasn't able to get past the shooting and the killing, then I ought to dust off my petticoats and go back behind my desk.'

'You'll be fine,' Macahan assured her. 'Hell, C.H. never would've taken a chance on you if he wasn't damn' sure you had enough salt for the job — 'specially knowin' you'd have to deal with pig-swillin' garbage like Fennedy here.' He looked disgustedly at the corpse, adding: 'How long you been doggin' him any-ways?'

'Nigh on two months. Started back in Indian Territory. Almost caught up with him twice — once in Ingalls, then again in Sallisaw — but each time he must've smelled my breath and got away clean.'

'Well, he didn't get away clean this time,' Macahan said. He looked at Drifter as if seeing him for the first time, and then turned back to the woman. 'You need to take the body back with you, Liberty?'

'Uh-uh. But I'd be obliged if you'd verify it's Fennedy for me.' She took out a creased piece of paper, unfolded it to reveal the dead man's face on a wanted poster and gave it to Macahan. 'That way, I can wire our office in Guthrie that Fennedy's dead and be on my way home.'

Macahan hunkered down and com-pared the poster to the face of the dead man. The corpse's stubbly beard was shorter, but otherwise the faces were identical. 'No disputin' it,' he said. 'It's Henry Fennedy.' Taking a stubbly pencil from his pocket, he licked the end and signed the wanted poster before handing it back. 'Oh'n next time you see C.H., Liberty, be sure'n give him my best.'

'Be glad to, Ezra.' Liberty folded the poster and returned it to her pocket. As she did, she half-turned toward Drifter. It was his first glimpse at her face. He was pleasantly surprised. She looked nothing like he expected. For one thing she was older than he'd thought — in her mid-thirties at least. From his angle he could not see if she was wearing any kind of star or badge, but from her conversation she was obviously some kind of law officer. Yet if he'd had to guess what she did for a living, he would have said store clerk, dressmaker, or maybe even a schoolteacher. She wasn't dainty or innocent-looking, but neither was there a trace of hardness to her; not about her full-lipped mouth or even in her sun-strained gray eyes. Despite smudges of trail dirt and straggly wisps of butter-colored hair poking out from under her sweat-stained hat, she was feminine enough for him to picture her in a dress.

She must have found him equally appealing because she held his gaze for several moments, lips pursed, eyes full of curiosity, before turning to the crowd. 'One of you folks go fetch the undertaker.'

'Ol' man McCormack, he's most likely asleep,' someone replied.

'Then wake him up. Drag him out of bed if you have to. But get him here!' Turning back to Macahan, she said, 'This town got a sheriff?'

'Of sorts.'

'Ahh,' said Liberty. 'So I shouldn't expect to see him any time soon, that what you're saying?'

'Not from what I hear, no.'

'Fair enough. Local law only gets in my way mostly, anyway.' She thumbed at Rosario's Cantina behind them, adding, 'Once Fennedy's in his box, be happy to spring for a drink.'

'It's on me,' Macahan said, adding, 'Better yet, it's on him.' He thumbed at Drifter, who grinned and said, 'Be my pleasure.' Then offering his hand to the woman, 'Quint Longley, ma'am.'

'Liberty,' she said.

'*Deputy US Marshal* Liberty,' added Macahan. 'From Guthrie.'

'Norman,' she corrected. 'I just work out of Guthrie.' She shook Drifter's hand firmly. 'Glad to know you, Mr Longley.'

12

No more than ten minutes had passed when Emily entered Rosario's Cantina. The small, low-ceilinged bar was noisy and smoky and she had to stand by the door for a few moments, looking over the crowd, before she spotted Drifter seated at a bench-table near the back door. He looked worried when he saw her approaching and, rising to greet her, demanded to know what was wrong.

'Nothing,' she replied. 'But I heard the shooting and when you didn't come back — '

'Didn't Lars tell you where I was?'

'Mr Gustafson was busy,' Emily said, amused.

'Doin' what?'

'Trying to convince *Mrs* Gustafson that he hadn't been drinking. Seems she didn't quite believe his story that during your game of checkers a cat knocked a bottle of whiskey off a shelf in the stable, causing it to break and spill all over her husband.'

'Aw Jesus,' Drifter said, grinning; while behind him, at the table, Macahan and Liberty started laughing.

'Hell,' Liberty said, 'don't matter if it's true or not. Any fella who can rustle up a lie like that deserves to be forgiven.'

'You ain't met Mrs Gustafson,' Drifter chuckled. 'She's no bigger'n than a ladybug but tough as yesterday's steak.'

Macahan, who'd been studying Emily, now stood up and offered her his chair. 'Will you join us, ma'am?'

Emily started to say no, then decided Macahan was too handsome to stay mad at and said, 'Thank you, Marshal. Believe I will.' She walked around behind Liberty, waited for Macahan to push her chair in and then sat down.

Scowling, Drifter sat across from her. 'You ain't gettin' no whiskey,' he said. 'So get that notion right out of your head.'

'You must be her pa,' Liberty said to Drifter.

'I am that.'

'Recently,' reminded Emily. 'Don't forget to add in that little fact.'

'Mean you were raised by another family?' Liberty said.

'The Mercers, yes.'

'Then we have something in common. I never knew my folks. I was found on a whore's doorstep. She cared for me for a spell, then, when she was run out of town, I sort of ran wild until the nuns took over. Now quit being a loud fart in an empty barrel,' she said to Drifter, 'and let the young lady have a snort.'

Emily beamed. 'Thank you, Marshal . . . uh . . . ?'

'Liberty.'

'Liberty what?'

'Just Liberty.'

' — Liberty. I can see we're going to get along just fine. Don't worry, Daddy,' she said to the still-scowling Drifter, 'this isn't the first time I've had a drink. Strict as the sisters were at St Marks, they couldn't watch us every second of every day.'

'Sneaked a bottle in now and then, did you?' Liberty said, laughing. 'My, my, shades of my days at Immaculate Heart. I swear I can still feel Sister Florentine's pointer 'cross my knuckles.' She drained her glass, refilled it from the half-empty bottle of whiskey on the table and handed the glass to Emily. 'To all that's holy.'

'Amen,' Emily said and gulped down the whiskey. She grimaced as it burned her throat but to her credit, or discredit, did not gag or choke.

'Enjoy that, did you?' Drifter asked her.

'Tolerable.'

'Good, 'cause that's your limit.'

Emily eyed him for a moment, saw something in his eyes that warned her not to defy him, and shrugged. 'So be it.' She turned to Liberty, who earlier had removed her duster, revealing a Deputy US Marshal's star pinned on her shirt. 'I didn't know there were any female deputy marshals?'

'Liberty's the first,' Macahan said.

'Third,' Liberty corrected. 'Mamie Fossett and a gal named Miller who works Indian Territory — they were appointed ahead of me.'

'Third or twenty-third,' Emily said with admiration, 'it's still a great achievement. You know,' she added to Drifter, 'I've never really settled on what I'd like to be one day, but being a deputy marshal sounds very appealing.'

Drifter almost erupted. But gritting back his anger, he said grimly, 'I don't reckon that was what Pa Mercer had in mind when he paid for your schoolin' at St Marks — '

'I'm sure it wasn't,' Emily said. 'He was a man who placed high value on education and integrity, not to mention the importance of the support of a good family. But sometimes good intentions, like good deeds, don't work out like we plan. And so long as I make something of myself, something that doesn't fly in the face of the Good Book, I'm sure Pa

Mercer — and Momma — would be proud of me.'

'You talk like they've passed,' Liberty said.

'They have. Along with both my stepbrothers, they were murdered by Comancheros.'

'Sorry.'

'It's all right,' Emily said. 'Still hurts, and guess it always will, but at least I've got my real father' — she pressed her hand over Drifter's hand and squeezed fondly — 'and that helps make up for most of it.'

Drifter smiled and felt warm inside. 'Reckon it's time we called it a night,' he said, rising. 'Got an early ride ahead of us tomorrow.' He looked at Macahan. 'Sunup.'

Macahan nodded. Then waiting until Drifter and Emily had said goodbye to Liberty and were walking to the door, he finished his drink and corked the bottle. 'C'mon,' he told Liberty. 'I'll walk you back to the hotel.'

Rising, she said, 'Where're you and

75

Longley riding to?'

'See a man about a lynching.'

'Sounds interesting. Want company?'

'Thought you were headed home?'

'Ahh,' Liberty said, smiling. 'Like Marshal Thompson's always saying: 'Home is where the lead flies'.'

Macahan gave a rare smile. 'Ol' C.H.,' he said. 'Ain't he a hoot?'

13

Latigo awakened to the sound of roosters crowing. He moved stiffly, his roped limbs cramped and numb from lack of circulation. He tried to move his fingers but they wouldn't respond and he soon gave up. His shoulders and back were chafed from constant rubbing against the support-post he was tied to, the pain strangely welcome compared to the numbness everywhere else. He could vaguely feel his legs, though not his feet, and he wondered if he could stand or walk, if by some miracle he did manage to escape.

He could now hear voices outside as the ranch-hands stumbled out of the bunkhouse. He looked toward the nearest stall, trying to see if the man guarding him was asleep. But everything appeared blurred and out-of-focus.

He blinked several times, his strange amber-colored eyes raw from lack of sleep. Both were sore and swollen from Slade Stadtlander's punches, delivered last night shortly after supper, while the Iverson brothers gleefully egged him on.

If he ever lived through this, Latigo thought grimly, he would kill all three of them, shooting each one in the belly to ensure they died slowly and painfully. He hated Slade and always had, even when he was ramrod of the Double S. But then he was not alone. Most people in Santa Rosa hated him, but were too afraid of his powerful, vindictive father to let their feelings show.

Stadtlander's only son, named for his dead mother's older brother, did not look like his father; nor did he have any of his few good traits: grit, faith in himself, and a refusal to quit no matter the odds. Instead Slade was a sly, mealy-mouthed bully known in the sleazy saloons and brothels along Lower

Front Street for beating up whores and drunks unable to defend themselves, usually with the help of his pals, Mace and Cody Iverson.

And now, Latigo thought, as he saw the silvery light of dawn glinting through cracks in the plank-walls of the big barn, Slade and the Iversons would have the last laugh; they were going to get to mock him as he hung there, kicking and twisting at the end of a rope.

And there was not one damned thing he could do about it.

14

It was a dawn to remember. Once the sun had cleared the distant mountain peaks to the east, its pale primrose light crept over the vast open scrubland and then gradually spread across the flat rooftops of the numerous adobe buildings scattered throughout Santa Rosa.

Good as his word, Lars Gustafson had a horse saddled for Macahan when at sunup the deputy marshal entered the stable, Liberty alongside him.

'Been a change of plans,' he told Drifter who stood with Emily and the old Swede just inside the doorway. 'Manager at the Carlisle says Stadtlander will most likely get off the train where the spur hooks up with the main line. Says that switch-point is closer to his ranch, so why ride the train all the way into town an' add extra miles to his journey?'

'Makes sense,' agreed Drifter, ' — 'cept the Sunset don't stop there.'

'It will for him,' Macahan said. 'That old devil may not own the Southern Pacific, but you can bet your saddle he knows Huntington an' them other railroad barons that do.'

'I don't like it,' Emily said as if asked. 'If for some unknown reason Mr Stadtlander doesn't get off, and we miss him, he could reach his ranch ahead of us and hang Lat before we can stop him.'

Macahan didn't respond. But his expression suggested that he didn't think hanging Latigo was the worst thing he'd ever heard of, and certainly not something he was going to lose sleep over. 'Let's get some trail behind us,' he said to Drifter, who nodded. Both men went to their horses.

Liberty, who'd been quietly rolling a smoke, now stuck it between her lips, flared a match on her gunbelt and lit the pinched end. 'This is none of my business, mind,' she said quietly to

Emily, 'but Ezra tells me you've got feelings for this Latigo fella — that true?'

'Yes. Why?'

'Well, no offense, but you look smarter than that. I mean, this is the first time I've had cause to track an outlaw outside of Oklahoma or Indian Territory, but even back there me and every lawman I know has heard of Latigo Rawlins — and I gotta tell you, little sister, what we've heard is mostly all bad.'

'I'm not denying that,' Emily said defiantly. 'But as I've already told my father and the marshal, no matter what Lat has done, or what the law eventually has in store for him, he does not deserve to be lynched. No one does. And that's all I have to say about it.' She spun around, marched to her horse, mounted, and, head held high, eyes straight ahead, guided the blue roan stallion out of the barn.

Astride the sorrel Drifter watched as she rode out, then he sighed and shook his head at Macahan and Liberty. 'I've been known to be stubborn in my time,' he said, exasperated, 'but compared to my daughter, hell, I'm the town roundheels.'

Macahan grunted as if he agreed with him.

Liberty didn't. 'I admire Emily,' she said. 'I don't agree with her choice in men, but if I'd had her guts and determination, I would've been a deputy marshal years ago. Instead I sat quietly behind a sewing machine, hating myself, listening to all those naysayers who convinced me a woman had no right to be a lawman.'

'Well, you're a deputy now,' Macahan said, 'an' a damn' good one to boot.'

'Yeah,' Liberty said. 'But I had to *wait* ten years 'fore a man decided it was all right for me to be one. *That's* what galls me.'

★ ★ ★

When the four of them reached Dome Rock, where the spur joined the main line from Deming, there was no sign of the train. The sun was now fully up and blazed like a white fire in the cloudless blue sky. Dismounting beside the switch-lever, which was padlocked, they loosened their saddle-cinches and drank from their canteens, the water almost as hot as the dry, rose-colored desert stretched out on all sides them.

'If the stationmaster's right,' Macahan said, checking his fob watch, 'train's due to pass by here in 'bout twenty minutes, give or take.'

'Let's hope it wasn't early today,' Emily said acidly, 'for all our sakes.'

Unfazed by her sarcasm Macahan removed his hat, mopped his brow with his neckerchief and then wiped the inner hat-band dry before returning the hat to his head. 'Funny you should say that, ma'am,' he said laconically. 'Me, now, I was hopin' it wouldn't be late. Just goes to show you, don't it, how opposite two personalities can be?' Hunkering down in the shade made by his horse, he dug out the makings and started to roll a cigarette.

'I could learn to really dislike that man,' Emily confided to her father. 'I swear he deliberately goes out of his way to irritate me.'

'And you him,' Drifter said, stifling a chuckle. 'Why is that, Daughter mine?'

Emily reddened as if offended. 'I don't know what you're talking about,' she said huffily. She stalked off and stood beside the sun-brightened tracks, staring into the distance.

Amused, Liberty joined Drifter, who was warily letting his moody, ill-tempered sorrel drink out of his cupped hands. 'Seems to me,' she said, 'we got one of those 'opposites attract' things goin' on here.'

Drifter rolled his eyes. 'I can only hope.'

'Yeah,' Liberty said, eyeing Macahan. 'She could do a lot worse.'

'Look! There it is,' Emily said, pointing.

Even as she spoke the others heard the faint, familiar sound of a far-off train whistle. As one, they looked toward the north-west and in the distance, just below the mountains that made up the horizon, could see a twist of black smoke spiraling upward.

''Be damned, Miss Emily, if you wasn't right after all,' Macahan needled. 'That sonofabuck *is* early!'

15

When the train was still more than a mile away, Drifter spotted a buckboard escorted by five riders approaching from the direction of Stadtlander's ranch.

'Got company,' he told the others. Taking field glasses from his saddle-bags he trained them on the riders. 'Figures . . . '

'A dollar says they're Double S riders,' Macahan said, squinting in the sunlight.

'You'd win that bet,' Drifter said. He handed the glasses to Macahan. 'Slade, the Iverson brothers an' a couple of hands — plus another handlin' the wagon.'

'Mr Stadtlander must've wired his son that he was getting off here,' Emily said.

'Slade, or that smarmy piece of crud

posin' as a sheriff,' Drifter said disgustedly, ' 'bout the same thing.'

Liberty added a sixth cartridge to her Colt, holstered it and then pulled her carbine from the saddle boot. 'Want me to go brace 'em,' she asked Macahan, 'so you can talk to this Stadtlander fella alone?'

'Nah. Slade an' the Iversons are all mouth.' He spat contemptuously. 'Can't say as I like the old man, but he's got more sand in his pants than them three yahoos put together. Tell you what you can do, though — keep an eye on the men that Stadtlander's brung with him. I don't want some young punk shootist decidin' this here's the time to make a name for hisself — at my expense.'

'Consider it done,' Liberty said.

Macahan turned to Drifter and Emily. 'Be 'bliged if you'd stay out of this till I see how Stadtlander intends to play me.'

'Bastard only knows one way,' Drifter growled, 'ride roughshod over everyone in his way.'

'Even so, I like to give a man enough rope to hang hisself. Sorry,' he said to Emily. 'Poor choice of words.'

She shrugged, but didn't say anything.

Drifter said, 'Tell you what, *amigo*, while we're stayin' out of it, we'll also make damn' sure Slade an' his men stay out of it too. How's that sound?'

'Dandy,' Macahan said. He turned back to the train. It was now close enough to count the bars on its cow-catcher, and already the engineer and brakemen were applying the brakes.

The Double S riders and the buckboard were also getting close. Drifter removed the safety strap keeping his Colt snug in the holster and stepped in front of Emily. 'Any shootin' starts,' he said, 'stay behind me.'

'Will you quit treating me like a little girl?' she said indignantly.

'Dammit, Emily! Don't give me any sass. I'm your father. Just do as I tell you.'

'First off,' she said, eyes blazing, 'as

I've told you before: being my father doesn't give you the right to order me around. And secondly, I think I proved in Mexico — and especially in Blanco Canyon — that I can look after myself. *And* make smart decisions. So thank you for worrying about me,' she added, softening. 'I appreciate it and love you for it. But if any of these Double S boys start shooting, believe me, Daddy, I intend to shoot back.'

Drifter sighed, frustrated and yet simultaneously proud. 'Just don't miss,' he grumbled.

'I don't intend to.' Emily caught Liberty looking over her shoulder at her. There was both amusement and respect in her gray eyes. Emily held her gaze for a moment and then winked.

Liberty smiled and faced front again, rifle crooked across her arm, her free hand hanging loosely beside her cedar-grip six-gun.

Macahan stood still as a statue, eyes fixed on the approaching train, his right boot resting on the near rail. The ground trembled underfoot as the train slowed to a shuddering, steam-hissing stop.

The conductor jumped down from the caboose, carrying a wooden box-step, and hurried toward the nearest passenger car. On reaching the small open platform at the end of the car, he set the step down and stood back so that two sour-faced gunmen could get off. Armed with six-shooters and shotguns, they surveyed the area for any sign of trouble.

The sight of Deputy US Marshal Macahan approaching, and behind him Drifter, Emily and Liberty standing holding rifles, made them uneasy.

The bigger of the two reboarded the train and spoke to someone in the passenger car. He reappeared a few moments later, followed by two other gunmen, who formed a protective half-circle around the exit platform.

A well-dressed rancher in his late sixties appeared behind them. Though short, stumpy and hampered by arthritis, his square, jut-jawed face, defiant steely gaze, pugnacious chin and thin-lipped mouth warned everyone that Stillman J. Stadtlander was no one to be messed with. He descended each step carefully, as if not trusting his legs to support him, irritably swatting aside any help offered by the gunmen, instead relying on a silver-handled mahogany walking stick to assist him off the box-step.

Once on the gravelly dirt beside the tracks, he focused his stare on Macahan, who now pushed aside two of the gunmen and confronted him.

''Mornin', Mr Stadtlander.'

'Marshal . . . ' The old rancher grinned tauntingly. 'Now why ain't I surprised to see you here?'

'Figured that's why you bought yourself a new sheriff,' Macahan said affably, 'to keep you updated on all the latest news.'

Stadtlander chuckled, more amused than angry. 'You know better than to suggest somethin' like that, Marshal. Salting an election, why that's pure illegal.'

'So they tell me, sir.'

'Must say it's mighty good of you to come all the way from El Paso to welcome me home.'

'Just tryin' to be neighborly,' Macahan said, adding, 'By the way, how's your gout doin'?'

'Runnin' a close second to my arthritis, if you want the truth. Hell of a thing, ain't it?' Stadtlander said, glaring at his misshapen legs. 'Man like me needin' to be helped off a train like a hundred-year-old granny.'

'Mr Stadtlander,' Macahan said, 'there ain't no man in this world less like a hundred-year-old granny than you, sir.' Then as the old gray-haired rancher chuckled: 'Now, how 'bout we quit strokin' each other's beard an' get down to why I'm really here.'

All the humor vanished from Stadtlander's tough weathered face. It was replaced by a grim, ruthless expression that would have alarmed a lesser man.

'Glad to, Marshal. But if we're cuttin' straight to the meat, you should know that nothin' you can say is gonna change my mind 'bout stringin' up Latigo Rawlins. Ungrateful, lyin' sonofabitch, he's made folks think I'm a murderer an' cost me a fortune in lawyers' fees besides, an' I still ain't out of hot water.'

'An' throwin' a noose on him is gonna solve all that?'

'Hell no! But sure as bunnies shit, it's gonna make me feel better.'

'But at what cost?'

'Reckon that's up to you.'

Macahan sighed. 'Then I guess we've both inherited a pile of trouble.'

'Mean you're actually gonna try to stop me?'

'I *am* gonna stop you, sir.'

'Don't be a goddamn' fool,' Stadtlander snarled. 'Countin' these boys I got fifty guns willin' to shoot holes in you — you *an'* that group of miserable misfits standin' behind you! By God,' he added, as if suddenly seeing Liberty, 'you lettin' petticoats wear a star these days? Jesus-Joseph-Mary, if I hadn't seen it with my own eyes . . . ' He shook his head as if lost for words.

Slade, the Iversons and the Double S hands started laughing.

Liberty showed no sign of hearing them.

'Funny thing,' Macahan drawled, loud enough to be heard above the panting hiss of the idling locomotive. 'Last night in Santa Rosa, I watched a killer named Fennedy bleed to death in the street.' He paused; then having caught everyone's attention, said, 'Seems outlaws die from Deputy Liberty's bullets same as ours.'

No one moved. No one spoke. The only sounds were the faint moaning of the wind mingled with the rhythmic hissing of the Iron Horse.

Stadtlander suddenly came to life. 'Son,' he barked at Slade, 'bring that damn' wagon over here!'

'Sure, Pa.' Slade used a length of woven rawhide looped around his wrist to whip the team and the startled horses lunged forward, almost unseating the driver.

Macahan turned and walked back to Drifter, Emily and Liberty. 'Mount up,' he told them. As one, they swung up onto their saddles and prepared to ride.

By now Slade had helped his father onto the buckboard. 'For the last time, Marshal,' Stadtlander growled, 'stay out of this. Prod me, an' I swear on my dead wife's grave, you'll cause more bloodshed than ten Latigos are worth!'

Macahan ignored him. But the old rancher's words weren't lost on him. 'I hate to admit it,' he told the others, 'but for once that ol' bastard might be tellin' the truth.'

'That mean you're going to let Lat hang?' Emily demanded.

'No,' Deputy US Marshal Macahan said grimly. 'But it *does* mean,' he added, addressing Drifter, 'if you're any kind of father, you'll make sure Emily gets safely back to town.'

'Only way that'll ever happen,' she said, before Drifter could answer, 'is if he shoots me and ties me face-down across my saddle.'

16

It was almost noon and the stifling heat inside the barn was intolerable. Even the flies buzzing around Latigo's head seemed drowsy.

Suddenly he heard the hands shouting excitedly to one another outside and wondered if it had anything to do with him. Not that it mattered. Though he'd furtively struggled all night to untie the rope binding his hands behind the support-post, the knots remained secure. He'd had a moment of hope about an hour ago when he thought he could feel the rope itself loosening; but then he realized it was just slippery from the blood coming from his chafed wrists . . . and he was finally forced to admit that without a knife or something equally sharp to cut the rope, he had little hope of escaping.

The ranch-hand guarding him, a tall,

gaunt, gloomy man known as Preacher, also heard the shouting. He closed the Bible he'd been reading, crossed himself and hurried outside. When he returned a few minutes later he looked sad and remorseful.

'Boss is comin',' he intoned. 'Time to say your prayers, Shorty.'

Latigo, who'd killed more than one man for calling him that, grinned mirthlessly. 'Prayin's a flat waste of time.'

'Why's that?'

''Cause there ain't no God to hear me.'

Preacher sadly shook his head. 'I pity you, brother. You're one sorry, lost soul.'

'Why, 'cause I don't believe in all that hogwash 'bout God or the hereafter or turnin' the other cheek?'

'Ain't hogwash, brother. It's straight from the Good Book an' there can't be no arguin' with that.'

'Why not? Bible's nothin' more'n a bunch of tall tales told by some religious freaks chewin' the fat 'round a fire.'

Aghast at Latigo's blasphemy, Preacher momentarily couldn't find words to reprimand him. His Adam's apple bobbed in his turkey-like neck as he gulped for air. Finally, he said solemnly, 'If it's any solace, brother, I'll pray for you when your time comes.'

His words had a strange effect on Latigo. Abruptly, he bowed his head and started sobbing.

Preacher frowned, puzzled. Moving closer, he asked, 'What is it, brother?'

'I . . . I'm scared of dyin',' Latigo said brokenly.

'Don't be, brother. You have nothin' to fear from the Lord. He forgives everyone their sins. Invites them into His arms and heart with no malice or — '

'P-Please,' Latigo begged. 'Pray for me, Preacher. Your soul is pure. Perhaps a few kind words from you would make God realize that it was just fear, fear of hangin', of the rope tightenin' 'bout my neck that made me lash out against

Him. Will you do that for me, Preacher?' Latigo looked up, eyes teary and raw from lack of sleep. 'Will you? Will you? I know I've killed men and I got no right to ask for forgiveness, but maybe if you pray for me, then God will forgive me an' save me from burnin' in the fires of Hell.'

Preacher saw the fear in the little blond Texan's amber-colored eyes and took pity on him.

'Of course, brother,' he said, kneeling in front of Latigo. 'Who am I to refuse a fellow Christian — '

His speech was cut off as Latigo, with every ounce of remaining strength, swung his legs up and kicked him under the chin. The pointed toe of one boot drove into the soft flesh, drawing blood, while the force of the kick snapped Preacher's head back, knocking him senseless. He collapsed, body crumpling half on the floor and half across Latigo's ankles.

'Amen,' Latigo murmured. Gripping the post between his elbows, he twisted his legs sideways in an effort to drag the body around behind him. Earlier he'd seen a sheath knife, with a buck-horn handle, hanging from Preacher's belt, and now he struggled desperately to push the unconscious man close to his hands.

It took him what seemed an eternity but finally his numbed fingers felt the pressure of the body pressed against them. He worked them frantically, hoping to feel the handle of the knife. Sweat poured down his face as he clawed around, unable to turn his head far enough around to see behind the post.

He groped blindly for several more minutes. 'C'mon, c'mon,' he urged himself. Then finally he felt the outline of the knife handle. With a gasp of joy, he forced his numb fingers to grasp it. It took great effort but once he had a firm grip, he lifted up his hands, slowly pulling the blade out of the sheath.

As he worked, Latigo could hear the men whooping it up outside. Mingled in with their shouting were the sounds of approaching horses and creaking wagon wheels.

Stadtlander had finally arrived!

Desperate, Latigo jerked the tip of the blade clear of the sheath and then for a moment, just sat there, motionless, heart pounding, trying to gather himself. Then twisting his wrists sideways, he started sawing the ropes with the blade — only to realize he was holding the knife so that the sharp edge was turned outward. Frustration raged through him. Finally managing to control himself, he slowly and carefully — lest he drop the knife — turned the blade over and again started sawing at the ropes.

But his chance of escape was doomed. At that moment the double-doors swung open and men, silhouetted against the bright sunlight, came crowding in. Slade and the Iverson brothers, Mace and Cody, eagerly led the way. When they saw Preacher lying unconscious on the floor behind the post and realized what Latigo was doing, they angrily crowded around him and began kicking him until he dropped the knife and slumped over in pain.

'Quit it! Leave him alone, damn you!'

When Slade and the men ignored Macahan's command, he fired a shot in the air — freezing everyone.

'Now back off,' he said, 'else the next bullet will bite more'n air!'

Slade and the others grudgingly pulled back from Latigo.

'You're makin' a mistake stickin' your nose in this,' Slade snarled at the lawman. 'You heard my ol' man — he's gonna string Latigo up an' there ain't nothin' you can do about it.'

'Sure there is. I can shoot you an' him, along with anyone else who butts in' — Macahan included the Iversons in his stare — 'all in the name of the law.'

'And I'll take care of any man Jack of you he misses,' said Liberty. She swung the carbine off her arm, levered in a shell and aimed the gun at Slade and his men, making them flinch. 'Also in the name of the law.'

Slade licked his lips nervously and tried to assume a swaggering posture, but failed miserably.

'If you think anyone 'round here's scared of buckin' the law, think again. My pa's the only law on the Double S an' *he* says Latigo swings.'

Macahan turned to Drifter, who stood with Emily beside him. 'Cut him loose.'

Drifter nodded, lowered his rifle but kept his finger on the trigger and started toward Latigo.

Bristling, Slade and the Iversons inched their hands toward their six-guns.

'Go ahead,' Drifter said when they didn't draw. 'Not often I get a chance to kill a weasel legally.'

'You ain't the law,' Mace Iverson sneered.

'Wrong,' Macahan said. 'I swore him in 'fore we left town.'

Drifted smiled thinly at Slade. 'Your call — *junior.*'

Slade's hand hovered over his six-gun.

All was quiet save for the faint buzzing of the ever-circling flies.

Macahan, his voice barely above a whisper, said, 'Emily . . . whyn't you do the honors.'

For an infinitesimal moment Emily was too surprised to move. Then pleased that Macahan had trusted her, she stepped between him and her father, walked around behind the post, picked up the horn-handled sheath knife and cut the ropes binding Latigo.

No one else moved.

Giving Latigo the knife to free up her hands, Emily draped one of his arms over her shoulder, slipped her free hand around the little Texan's waist and supporting most of his weight, assisted him out of the barn.

Macahan and Liberty — still facing Slade and his men — backed slowly toward the open double-doors.

Slade, already white with gritted rage, couldn't find the guts to stop them or to draw on Drifter.

'Either jerk that iron,' Drifter told him, 'or unbuckle your gunbelt.'

Slade wanted to draw so badly his right hand quivered, but he couldn't get past his fear.

Drifter laughed. 'Tell you what — I'll make it easy for you,' and started to turn his back on him.

Instantly two things happened — both so quickly they appeared to happen together.

Slade went for his gun.

Drifter whirled around, and before Slade's gun cleared leather he slammed the young Stadtlander across his face with the rifle.

Slade crumpled to the straw-strewn floor. Lay there motionless.

Drifter eyed the Iversons and the other hands. 'Throw your guns in the corner. Do it!' he said, when they hesitated, 'else I got a legal right to shoot you.'

As one, they sullenly obeyed him.

'Now, get outside.'

Again they sullenly obeyed him.

Drifter reached down, grabbed Slade by the back of his shirt-collar and dragged him to the door.

17

Outside in the bright sunlight Macahan, Liberty and Emily, who was still supporting Latigo, found themselves confronted by about thirty men, all armed with rifles and six-guns.

Stadtlander stood glowering in front of them, supporting himself with his walking stick.

'All right, Marshal,' he growled. 'You got your wish. Now make your play.'

'I already have,' Macahan replied. 'I got the prisoner I come for.'

'You'll never leave with him alive — none of you!'

'Possible.' Macahan paused as Drifter emerged from the barn dragging Slade, then said, 'But, stubborn as I know you are, sir, you ain't fool-headed. You didn't bust your tail all these years buildin' a spread like this to die knowin' there was no one to leave it to.'

Stadtlander chewed on that for a moment then looked at his son, who lay still, unconscious at Drifter's feet. 'I take it he ain't dead?'

He was talking to Drifter, who shook his head. 'Not yet.'

'You expectin' me to make a swap, Marshal — Latigo for my son?'

'Seems reasonable.'

'You ever heard anyone call me reasonable?'

'Can't say as I have,' Macahan said. 'But I haven't ever heard anyone call you stupid, neither, so I'm bettin' you ain't.'

'You willin' to die to find out?'

Macahan brushed a fly from his nose before saying, 'If I wasn't, sir, I never would've let 'em pin this star on me.'

Slade now stirred groggily beside Drifter.

Stadtlander eyed his son somewhat unfavorably and then looked at Latigo, who was still leaning on Emily's shoulder.

'You said 'prisoner', Marshal — what's

that mean exactly?'

'I'm takin' Rawlins to Santa Rosa, where I'm lockin' him up till the circuit judge arrives. Then he'll stand trial for murderin' those Mexican ranchers.'

'In other words, he gets a rope either way?'

'That's not for me to decide. My job ends at the courtroom door.'

'P-Pa . . . '

All eyes turned to Slade, now shakily sitting up and looking at his father.

'You ain't lettin' them take him, are you?'

'Sooner die, would you?'

Slade struggled to his feet and stood there, swaying unsteadily.

'They're bluffin', Pa. Can't you see that?'

'My boy's got a point,' Stadtlander said to Macahan. 'Thirty of us, four of you. I'd bluff in your position.'

'Only he's not bluffin',' Drifter said, pressing his rifle against Slade's head. 'None of us is.'

'What've you got to lose anyway?'

110

Macahan said. 'Even if the verdict ain't a rope, you'll be dead long before Latigo gets out of prison — if he ever gets out.'

'Pa — '

'Shut up!' Stadtlander barked. 'Try to act like you ain't got your head stuffed up your ass, for once.' Then to Macahan, 'All right, take him.'

Macahan nodded, his grim, tight-lipped expression never changing. Turning to Drifter, he indicated Slade. 'Bring him along.'

'No!' Stadtlander waved his stick angrily at the marshal. 'My boy stays or we start shootin'. An' that's no bluff.'

Macahan considered briefly. 'Have I got your word that your men won't follow us and try to take him back?'

'You have.'

'That's good enough for me.' Macahan nodded at Drifter, who removed his rifle from Slade's head.

'One last thing, Marshal,' Stadtlander warned. 'If for some reason — any reason — you don't deliver Latigo to the judge, or if the jury goes soft on him an' he walks out of that courtroom a free man, I'll be there, outside, with my boys an' a rope, to make damn' sure he don't see another sunset.'

'I wouldn't expect less,' Macahan said.

Satisfied, Stadtlander limped off, his men stepping back to allow him to pass through their ranks.

Macahan, Drifter and Liberty swapped looks of relief.

Emily and Latigo did the same.

'Let's go, Ezra,' Drifter urged, ''fore that ol' bastard changes his mind an' turns his guns on us.'

Macahan nodded and turned to Emily and Latigo. 'You two are gonna have to ride double.'

'Fine with me,' Emily said. She helped Latigo, who winced at every movement, to step up into the saddle; then, with a boost from Drifter, she swung up behind him.

Macahan moved alongside the roan stallion and unhooked his handcuffs from his belt. 'Give me one of your hands,' he told Latigo.

'Go on, Lat,' Emily said when Latigo didn't obey. 'Do as he says.'

Reluctantly, Latigo let Macahan cuff his left wrist and then lock the other cuff around the saddle horn.

Latigo eyed him sourly out of his swollen eyes. 'From one lynchin' to another, huh, Marshal?'

'Only this one's legal,' Macahan said coldly.

18

Stadtlander kept his word. They reached the outskirts of Santa Rosa without any interference from his son or his men. There, as the little party rode into town, Emily, who was riding with her arms around Latigo, felt him wince.

'What is it?' she asked, concerned. He grunted with pain and hunched forward over the stallion's neck. 'Lat . . . Lat, you all right?'

'Inside,' he said, teeth gritted. 'I'm all busted up. Hurts real bad.'

'Marshal . . . stop a minute!'

Macahan, Drifter and Liberty reined up, swung their horses around and rode back alongside Emily.

'What's wrong?' Macahan asked.

Latigo grunted something no one could understand.

'He's in a lot of pain,' Emily said.

'All that kickin' he took,' Drifter said,

'most likely broke some ribs.'

'One of them could've punctured his lungs, too,' Emily said. 'We have to get him to the doctor right away.'

'No,' Macahan said. 'First, jail. Then we'll bring the doc to him.'

'But what if he needs surgery? Then we'll have to carry him over to Dr Talbot's and . . . by then he could be . . . be . . . ' She stopped, unable to say the word 'dead'.

'No need to panic,' Latigo said, wincing as he straightened up. 'I'm not ready to go feet up just yet.'

'Satisfied?' Macahan asked Emily.

'Lat would say that even if he was dying,' she said. 'So would you and Daddy and most other men. Good heavens, you're all so afraid we women might think you aren't tough that — '

'Emily, for God's sake shut up,' Drifter said, not unkindly. He turned to Macahan. 'I'll ride ahead. Tell the doc to meet us at the jail.' He dug in his spurs and rode off before anyone could argue.

* * *

Later, when Macahan, Emily, Liberty and Latigo entered the sheriff's office, they found Drifter and Dr Talbot already there, awaiting them. Sheriff Wirter was also present. The rotund, pompous lawman insisted on being the one to actually lock Latigo in a cell, and then irritated everyone even further by refusing to allow Dr Talbot to examine Latigo before Macahan signed the official 'arrest' and 'prisoner transfer' forms.

'I'm sure you would do the same in my position,' he said as Macahan sat at his desk filling out the paperwork. 'After all, we as lawmen are duty-bound to follow official procedure — don't you agree, Marshal?'

Macahan gave him a baleful stare but chose not to answer. Instead he signed the documents, then without a word picked up the keys to the cells and led Dr Talbot back to examine Latigo.

Sheriff Wirter looked hurt. 'Do you

think I'm wrong to insist on following protocol, Deputy?' he asked Liberty, who sat beside Drifter and Emily.

'What I think,' Liberty replied, 'would give you heartburn. By the way,' she added, 'where were you the night I had to shoot Henry Fennedy? I mean, if this was my town, I'd sure as hell want to ask me a few questions about why I shot down a fella in the middle of Main Street and risked harming innocent bystanders!'

'If I'd been in town at the time of the shooting, naturally I would have done exactly that,' Sheriff Wirter said. 'But, unfortunately, I was attending to official business.'

'In other words,' put in Drifter, 'you were off playin' your damn' fiddle someplace?'

Stung, Sheriff Wirter's face grew red. 'Th-that's a lie!' he sputtered. 'I was with the mayor and — ' He stopped as the door leading to the cells opened and Macahan and Dr Talbot emerged.

Emily was instantly on her feet,

asking, 'How is he, Doctor? Are his ribs broken? Is he going to be all right?'

'He'll be fine — eventually,' Dr Talbot assured her. 'But one, possibly two, of his ribs are cracked or broken — it's hard to know which when there's swelling and he's in so much pain — and two others are badly bruised.'

'But he will heal?'

'If he does what I told him, yes. That is, to get plenty of rest and to avoid all vigorous physical activity for at least six weeks. By then, the ribs should have healed properly.'

'Gettin' rest won't a problem for him,' Macahan said, 'not where he's headed.'

Emily gave the deputy marshal an ugly look then said to the doctor, 'Is there anything you can do about the pain? He's hurting dreadfully.'

'Not much, I'm afraid, no.' Dr Talbot, a tall, slender man in his mid-forties with thinning brown hair, sounded ashamed. 'I rubbed what little morphine I had left over the injured area, but once that wears off he's going to find even breathing very painful.'

'A good slug of whiskey always helps,' Liberty said. 'I fractured one of my ribs once when this filly threw me — the doc I saw was from Europe someplace, I don't remember where, and he recommended I take a drink every few hours to help kill the pain so I could keep on breathing properly — said otherwise, if it hurt so bad I only took little breaths, my lungs might get infected.'

'It can also increase a person's chances of catching pneumonia,' Dr Talbot said, 'though none of my patients has ever experienced that.'

'May I see him?' Emily asked.

'It's me you should be asking,' Sheriff Wirter said testily. 'He's *my* prisoner and he's in *my* jail.'

'Only till next election,' Drifter said. 'By then folks will be so sick of your fiddlin' not even Stadtlander will be able to buy their votes.'

Sheriff Wirter flushed angrily. 'Keep provoking me, mister, and I will find a

119

reason to lock you up with Rawlins.'

Pissed, Drifter started toward him. But Macahan quickly stepped between them and motioned for him to back off. Then turning to the sheriff, he growled, 'You gonna 'blige this lady or not?'

Not anxious to tangle with Macahan, Sheriff Wirter picked up the jail keys and unlocked the door. 'You may have ten minutes with the prisoner, Miss Mercer.' He waited for Emily to enter then locked the door behind her and returned to his desk. 'Is there anything else, Marshal?'

'Yeah,' Macahan said. 'When Emily gets done talkin' to Latigo, tell her to meet us over at Rosario's.' He nodded for Drifter and Liberty to leave and then followed them out.

The sheriff moved to the window, watched as the three of them started across the street and then went and sat behind his desk. There, he opened his fiddle case, lovingly took out his fiddle and began playing 'The Arkansas Traveler'.

19

Despite the excruciating pain that pierced his ribcage every time he breathed, Latigo insisted on standing in his cell as he talked to Emily through the bars. 'You gotta believe me,' he said. 'No matter what your pa or anyone else tells you, they're goin' to hang me!'

'Lat, please — '

'No, just listen, dammit! I know what I'm talkin' about. That scum-bucket of a sheriff told me, right to my face while he was lockin' me in here — said I was his ticket to gettin' re-elected. Kept taunting me 'bout it. Said folks would remember him favorably for stringin' up a cold-blooded murderer.'

'Who cares what he said? It's not up to him,' Emily said, 'it's up to a judge and a jury — '

'A jury made up of folks from around here — folks who are scared to cross

Stadtlander! An' we all know what that bastard wants — to watch me danglin' from a rope! I'm tellin' you, Emily, the only way I'm not gonna hang is if I break out of here.'

'Nonsense! There are legal ways to pick the right jury and then to sway them into your corner and a good lawyer knows how to do that.'

'Stadlander *owns* all the good lawyers,' Latigo said angrily. 'Don't you understand that, girl? Hell, I worked for the man — as his ramrod. I saw how he keeps them all on his payroll, whether he needs them or not, just so no one else can use them against him.'

'Maybe that's true here, or in Deming, or Las Cruces,' Emily admitted, 'but not in El Paso or Tucson or Phoenix. He doesn't own all the lawyers there. And that's where I'll go. From place to place, if necessary. And if I can't find a lawyer willing to represent you in one of those towns, I'll go elsewhere. Trust me, I'll find one even if I have to go as far as St Louis.'

'Emily — '

'No, no, I don't want to hear any more talk about hanging. You must have faith, Lat,' she added when he didn't respond. 'You have to believe in me. I can do this. I'm stubborn and determined and I won't let you down. I promise. The circuit judge won't be here for another two weeks and by then I *will* have found you a lawyer.'

'Even if you do,' Latigo said glumly, 'an' by some goddamn miracle he persuades the jury not to hang me, what then? I spend the rest of my days behind bars? Seein' you on visitin' days? Jesus, Emily, that's no life.'

'Maybe not. But it's better than a rope. Anything is. At least if you're alive, we can keep appealing, keep trying to get your sentence lessened.'

'Not so long as Sheriff Wirter's wearin' a star. Or Macahan for that matter. He hates my guts. Hell, you heard what he told Stadtlander at the ranch: that he'd be dead before I ever got out of prison. Nah,' he continued before Emily could say anything, 'the only thing that can save me from a rope is if you help me get out of here.'

'You mean break you out?'

'Exactly.'

'No,' she said. 'Even if I *could* do that, which isn't likely, that'd mean you — we would spend the rest of our lives on the run.'

''Least we'd be together.'

'Yes, but for how long? Days, weeks — at most, months? No, thank you.' Emily shook her head. 'I love you, Lat, and I'd do almost anything to help make a life for us, but I will not be the wife of an outlaw. That's where I draw the line.'

'Why?'

'Because that *is* no life. It's merely an existence. We'd have to hide out like bats in a cave, afraid of every sound we hear, or new person we meet, until eventually you get caught or killed. Where's the future in that? And I want a future. Oh, I may be young and still uninformed about a lot of things, but

I'm no different to any other woman: I want a husband, children, and a future.'

'How 'bout watching your husband dance from a rope?' Latigo said angrily. 'There any future in that?'

'That's unfair,' she began.

But Latigo had already turned away and, wincing, was limping to his cot. On reaching it, he gingerly sat down, leaned back against the wall and closed his eyes.

'Please, Lat,' she begged, 'let's not argue.'

He didn't respond.

'Let me try to find a lawyer . . . '

Again, no response.

'Lat, talk to me. Please . . . '

'Nothin' to talk about,' he said without opening his eyes. 'Not unless you're willin' to help me break out.'

'No,' she said firmly, 'I can't — won't do that. Ever. What's more, if you really loved me, like you say, you wouldn't want me to do it . . . wouldn't want me to break the law and maybe go to prison myself.'

It was what he'd been waiting for. 'Maybe I don't love you that much,' he said flatly. 'Ever thought of that?'

She hadn't. Nor did she want to.

Dismayed and hurting, she said, 'Please don't talk like that. I know you don't mean it. You can't. Not after all the things you've said, the promises you made, how you'd always look after me and — '

'I can't look after you while I'm in here,' he said, 'or in prison.'

'That's why you have to let me find you a lawyer — '

'Forget the damn lawyer, will you?' He broke off, wincing as he raised his voice, then said, 'All a lawyer can do is prolong the inevitable.'

'But — '

'I mean it, Emily. I don't intend to hang an' I sure as spit ain't spendin' the rest of my days in prison. Not for you, not for anyone!'

There was a grim bitterness to his voice she had not heard before. It stabbed her heart like a pointed icicle and she went cold all over.

'Very well,' she said sadly. 'If that's how you feel, I guess there's nothing more to say.'

'Reckon not.'

She waited, motionless, hoping for a last-second change of heart, but it never came. Suddenly she felt dead inside. Turning, she went to the door, knocked, and tearfully asked the sheriff to let her out.

* * *

Alone, Latigo sat there in the stifling heat, listening to the flies buzzing around his head, waiting to see if Emily returned. If he knew her as well as he thought he did, she wouldn't. When he'd first met her, he had sensed a pureness about her that would make it difficult if not impossible for her to lie or cheat or deliberately break the law — even for him. He'd counted on that when he'd asked her to help him escape. And she'd responded exactly as he guessed she would.

Time passed and still she did not return. He sighed, relieved. Losing Emily hurt worse than his injured ribs. But it was worth it. He'd never cared about any woman before and now he'd driven off the one he loved. Sounded loco, but at least he was sure that she wouldn't ruin her life by trying to help him break out. Now he was free to escape by himself.

Gritting his teeth against the intense pain, he gently lowered himself to the floor. Once there, he bit his lip until it bled. Then he reached down to his right boot and pulled out the horn-handled knife Emily had given him in Stadtlander's barn. Hiding it inside his shirt sleeve, he twisted his body to make it look like he had fallen off the cot. Then he cried out. When no one came, he cried out again . . . louder . . . and again . . . louder still . . . until finally the door was unlocked and Sheriff Wirter entered. Stepping up to the bars, he saw Latigo writhing in pain on the floor.

'What happened?' he demanded.

'I . . . I fell . . . Help me up,' Latigo begged. He turned his head toward the sheriff, so the lawman could see the blood on his lips. 'I . . . I'm bleedin' inside . . . my lungs maybe . . . Hurry,' he added, when the sheriff didn't move, ' 'fore I choke to death.'

'All right, all right . . . ' Grumbling, Sheriff Wirter reluctantly unlocked the cell, stepped inside and hunkered down beside Latigo. Sliding one arm under the little Texan, he leaned forward and started to lift him up — when suddenly Latigo rolled over and buried the knife in the lawman's belly.

Gasping, Sheriff Wirter desperately grabbed Latigo's hand and tried to force the bounty hunter to pull the knife out. But Latigo merely drove the blade deeper and upward, in one motion, gutting him.

Sheriff Wirter slumped back against the cot, both hands grasped about the knife, blood reddening his fingers.

Latigo grinned at him. ' 'Bout all

them votes you mentioned earlier
. . . still figure I'm your ticket to gettin'
re-elected?'

Sheriff Wirter didn't answer. He was
dead.

20

Making sure the outer office was empty, Latigo moved stiffly to the gun-rack. Every movement sent pain searing through him, accompanied by a troubling sense of nausea. But somehow he fought through it and, grabbing a rifle and a box of shells, he checked the drawers of the sheriff's desk. A gunbelt lay curled in the bottom one. Buckling it on, he picked up a half-empty bottle of whiskey that had been under the belt and took a long swig. It chased away the nausea and a second equally long swig helped deaden some of the pain. He was tempted to drain the bottle. But knowing he needed to stay alert, he resisted and instead tucked it in his jacket pocket and limped to the door.

That's when he saw the violin case leaned against the wall beside the desk. Impulsively, he limped over to it, picked it up and opened it. Inside was the sheriff's fiddle. Latigo grinned mirthlessly. Then he slammed the butt of the rifle down on the fiddle, splintering it into pieces. It didn't dampen the pain in his ribs, but it was music to his soul. He grunted, satisfied that he'd finally erased all his hatred for the sheriff, and limped out.

Outside, the sun-scorched street was filled with riders and horse-drawn wagons. Sweat-soaked townspeople trudged wearily about their daily routine. Latigo looked across the street. Drifter's sorrel, Macahan's gray, Liberty's bay and Emily's blue roan stallion, El Diablo, were tied up outside Rosario's Cantina. Teeth gritted, he walked as casually as he could across the street. No one seemed to notice him. Untying the stallion, he stuffed the Winchester under the scabbard holding Emily's rifle, grasped the horn and swung up into the saddle. Pain made him dizzy. For a moment he thought he might pass out. But he didn't. Steadying himself, he eased El Diablo away from the other horses and rode slowly on down the street.

Each jarring step the stallion took made Latigo grimace. But the thought of hanging enabled him to endure the agonizing pain and once he reached the edge of town, he kicked the roan into a steady lope and headed toward the Mexican border.

★   ★   ★

It was some twenty minutes later when Deputy Mel Gossett, a lazy, sleepy-eyed man not prone to panic, entered Rosario's and approached the plank table where Macahan sat drinking with Drifter, Emily and Liberty.

'Better come,' he said, so only they could hear. Then he was gone, striding out of the cantina before they could question him.

'Must be important,' Drifter said, draining his drink. 'That's the fastest I've ever seen Mel move.'

Outside, Emily realized her horse was

gone. Guessing Latigo had taken it, she said nothing but ran across the street with the others and entered the sheriff's office.

Sheriff Wirter's corpse was still slumped against the cot in Latigo's cell.

'That's how I found him,' Deputy Gossett told them. 'Dead as a Thanksgivin' turkey.'

Emily turned away, realizing that all hope of ever reuniting with Latigo was gone.

'Most likely halfway to Mexico by now,' Macahan said.

'Or already there,' Drifter said. Then as they looked at him, 'He's on El Diablo.'

'That right?' Macahan said to Emily. 'He stole your stallion?'

She nodded, hoping they didn't notice her tears.

'How come you didn't say so before?' Liberty demanded.

'What was the point?' Emily said. 'You'll never catch him, not on Diablo.'

'Oh, I'll catch him,' Macahan said

grimly. 'Maybe not today. Or tomorrow, or even next week. But I'll surely catch him. Just a matter of time an' time's the one thing I got plenty of.'

'I'll go with you,' Liberty said. 'But first I got to wire Marshal Thompson in Guthrie — get his say-so.'

'Count me in, too,' Drifter said.

'Better think twice on that,' Macahan said to both of them. 'I got no jurisdiction in Mexico.'

'Don't matter a hoot to me,' Drifter said.

'Me neither,' Liberty said. 'Hell, every time I go after someone in Indian Territory I don't have no jurisdiction. But I still go. Just means it's more likely my prisoner comes back face-down over the saddle.'

'You try to take Lat,' Emily warned, 'it'll be you who ends up face-down. Ask my father,' she added, looking at Drifter. 'He'll tell you. No one's faster than Latigo.'

Liberty chuckled. 'Thanks for the warning, honey. But don't worry about me. I don't intend on shooting it out with Rawlins or anyone else. I leave that kind of storybook nonsense to Ned Buntline and them other dime novel writers. Me, I make sure I got my man dead to rights 'fore I move in.'

'Reckon it's all set then,' Macahan said. 'Soon as we round up supplies, we start after him.'

'First, I'll need a horse,' Emily said to her father. 'Will you come with me to the livery stable — ask Mr Gustafson if I can use one of his?'

''Fore we do that,' Drifter said, 'better ask Ezra, here, if you're invited. It's his call.'

'Oh no, not again,' Emily grumbled. 'I'm always last dog out.' She faced Macahan. 'How about it, Marshal? Can I come along?'

'Depends.'

'On what?'

'Whose side you're on.'

'You mean will I try to help Lat escape if he's cornered?'

'Will you?'

Emily thought long and hard before answering. 'No.'

'Even if it comes to bloodshed?'

'No.'

'I got your word on that?'

'Yes. But,' she added after a pause, 'I want your word on something too.'

'I'm listenin'.'

'If it *does* come to bloodshed, promise me you'll give Lat a chance to surrender. You won't just shoot him down. I want your word too,' she said to Liberty. 'Otherwise, I'll try to find him on my own.'

''Fore I let that happen,' Drifter grumbled, 'I'll rope you to a damn' tree.' He looked at Macahan: 'Well? What's it goin' to be?'

Macahan turned to Liberty, who nodded, and then he said to Emily: 'Got our word.'

'Then may I ride with you?' Emily asked.

'Reckon so.'

21

Juanita Sanchez was one whore who did not have a heart of gold. But gold did play an important part in her life. For gold, whether it was jewelry or coin, she could be persuaded to do almost anything short of murder. It was her greed and cheerful lack of conscience that Latigo was counting on that afternoon when he rode into Los Locos, a small, dusty pueblo in the foothills of the sierras south of the border.

Known as a haven for *bandidos* and Yanqui renegades, the lawless town consisted of numerous narrow dirt streets lined with cantinas and adobe hovels inhabited mostly by people not welcome anywhere else. An ancient abandoned white church with a bell-less bell-tower, built by Spanish invaders, stood as a sort of shrine to the godlessness and evil that flourished there.

One of Juanita's numerous illegitimate children, Marta, saw him first. No more than five or six, depending on her mother's memory, she was sitting on the dirt between two potted cactuses that framed the front door, scolding a mangy dead kitten for not talking to her, when she heard a horse approaching. Looking up she noticed that the rider was slumped over the horse's neck, as if hurt or dying. But still he was a *gringo*, and *gringos* meant tortillas and beans on the table; so leaving the dead kitten to the flies, she ran indoors calling to her mother.

Though it was late afternoon Juanita was still asleep in bed. The bed was her pride and joy, not to mention her workplace. Originally owned by a former governor of Chihuahua, it had been stolen by *bandidos* while in transit to his ranchero and then given to Juanita by the bandit leader, Chico Perez — a ruthless, mercurial, fatly handsome rebel who was wild about her and bedded her every chance he got. It was a four-poster bed, made of brass, with a big jaguar-head knob atop each of the posts, and real springs under the mattress. The rhythmic squeaking the springs made while Juanita was pleasuring her customers was loud enough to be heard outside the thick adobe walls, the familiar sound alerting any potential customers that she was presently 'occupied'.

Now, as Marta vigorously shook her mother and told her to wake up, Juanita opened one eye and groggily demanded to know what her daughter wanted.

'*Gringo, gringo, gringo!*' Marta said shrilly.

'How many?'

'*Uno.*'

'Only one?' Juanita yawned, disappointed, and rubbed the sleep from her fiery black eyes. 'Well, I suppose one is better than none. Send him in, little one. Send him in.'

Her daughter didn't move.

'Why do you stand there, child? Do as I tell you. Send the *gringo* in. *Prisa, nino!*'

'But, Momma, it is him. The one! The *gringo* you call Señor Handsome.'

Immediately, Juanita lost all sleepiness. 'Latigo? He is here? In our village?' Jumping out of bed, she smoothed the covers, pulled on a bright red dress and then looked at her reflection in the gilt-framed mirror balanced on a shelf beside a marble crucifix. 'Are you sure it is him?'

'Yes, Momma. I see him coming. But he is much hurt, I think.'

'Hurt? *Madre de Dios*! Why do you not say this before?' She rushed out, leaving Marta making faces at herself in the mirror.

* * *

Macahan, Drifter, Emily and Liberty rode slowly across the border. Though dusk was settling, there was reason to hurry. As Emily had pointed out earlier, so long as Latigo was riding her tireless blue roan stallion, El Diablo, they were not going to catch him. Persistence, not haste, was their ally. Besides, in his condition, he could not ride too far without stopping. Also, before they left Santa Rosa Drifter had taken the two deputies aside and confided that he had a pretty good notion of where the injured little Texan might be headed. He hadn't mentioned this to Emily, he explained, because he had not wanted to hurt her, or have her accuse him of trying to denigrate Latigo's character at a time when she knew he hated the idea of her caring about Latigo, let alone considering marrying him, but it was well known that Latigo had a fondness for Mexican whores, and in particular for one named Juanita Sanchez. 'It's just a hunch,' Drifter admitted, 'but I'd bet my saddle that that's where we'll find him — Los Locos.'

'Then that's where we'll go first,' Macahan said. He scowled at the thought of Los Locos. 'If I had my way,' he added, filling his cheek with a fresh wad of chew, 'I'd round up all the best lawmen I knew an' clean out Los

Locos, 'long with all the other goddamn hellholes that straddle the border.'

'Marshal Thompson and I feel the same way 'bout most of the settlements and tent towns in Indian Territory,' Liberty said. 'They're nothing but breeding grounds for every outlaw and malcontent still festering 'bout the outcome of the war . . . all of them figuring the Union owes them a free piece of everything good and decent.'

Where they crossed the border there was no sign or difference in the landscape, or the windless heat, and but for a large rocky outcrop shaped like an eagle's head, which everyone familiar with the area used as a landmark, there was nothing to tell them they were entering Mexico.

They rode until dark. A sickle moon surrounded by a sprinkling of stars showed that the terrain was still mostly flat, with shallow gullies here and there, but in the distance now lumpy silhouettes verified they were approaching the foothills. They were now within a mile of Los Locos and Macahan decided they should make camp among some rocks, snatch a few hours of sleep and then enter town at sunup. 'That way,' he said to the three of them, 'if your hunch is right, Quint, we got a fair chance of catchin' Latigo while he's asleep.'

'What hunch?' Emily said. She looked at her father when no one answered her. 'What's going on? You hiding something from me?'

Drifter said quietly, 'There's a woman he likes. Lives in Los Locos. It's possible, maybe even likely, that Latigo went to her figurin' she might let him hole up with her while his ribs heal.'

'I see,' Emily said icily. 'And by woman, I suppose you mean — whore?'

'She's been known to entertain men,' Drifter conceded.

'Charming.'

'Now, sweetheart — '

'And just when were you going to mention this whore to me — *before* or *after* you dragged Lat out of her bed?'

'Take it slow,' Drifter said gently. 'No

144

need to get all riled up over somethin'
that may not even be true.'

'Riled up, did you say?' Emily
snorted angrily. '*Riled up!*'

'Daughter, please — '

'Oh, I am beyond being riled up,
Father! *Way beyond!* And why the devil
shouldn't I be? I mean, the man I love,
the man whom I got expelled for, a
man who claimed he loved me and
supposedly was willing to hang up his
guns and start a whole new life with
me, first asks me to help break him out
of jail and when I refuse, as good as
tells me to get out of his life. Then,
before I'm over that pleasant little
shock, he stabs a sheriff to death,
escapes and steals my horse — a horse
that means more to me than almost
anything — and where does he go?
Right into the arms of some Mexican
whore whom he's apparently known
— no, make that *cared about* since
heaven knows when and all along you,
Father, the one person I'm supposed to
trust and who is supposed to have my

best interests at heart, knew all about her but decided she wasn't worth mentioning. If that isn't humiliating enough, she's suddenly thrown in my face like a bucket of cold water and . . . and . . . now you expect me not to get *riled up*? Mary Mother of God, Daddy, what do you think I am — a marble statue with ice instead of blood in my veins?'

Drifter paled under her verbal onslaught, but could not think of anything to say — or anything that would not add fuel to the already inflamed feelings of his daughter.

But his silence only seemed to increase her rage. Tears of anger and frustration running down her tanned cheeks, she turned and stormed off into the night.

'Don't,' Liberty told Drifter as he started after her. 'Now ain't a good time. Let her be alone for a spell.'

Drifter grudgingly obeyed her advice, but his angst was clearly visible on his rugged, weathered face. 'Be mighty 'bliged if you'd talk to her when she's calmed down some,' he said wretchedly.

'Tell her I'm sorry an' that she's right: I didn't ought to have kept quiet about Juanita. Emily deserved to know. It's just that I figured she'd hate me for tellin' her an' — '

Liberty stopped him. 'I'll talk to her,' she said. 'See if she'll tell me what's really eating at her.'

'Reckon that's obvious, ain't it?'

'If you mean finding out about Latigo and this whore he knows, no — my guess is that's just the cream atop the milk. What's *really* eating at her goes much deeper than that. What it is I don't know. Maybe she don't even know what it is herself. Though, from listening to her, I'd say she's deep-down angry at something or someone other than Latigo.'

'Like who, for instance?'

Liberty shrugged. 'You'd have to ask someone a lot smarter'n me to get that answer. But if you want my gut feeling, I'd say it was either you or herself — or both — or maybe just the whole damn world in general.'

147

Drifter absorbed her words in pained silence.

'Reckon it's my fault,' Macahan said dismally. 'Never should've brung the subject up in front of her.'

'The hell you shouldn't,' Liberty said. 'That's what is at the bottom of all this, you ask me — folks she knows or loves keeping secrets from her.'

'You reckon?' Drifter said.

'I don't reckon,' Liberty said firmly. 'I know. I'm a woman, same as Emily, and folks — men in particular — have been treating me like a powder puff, pushing me aside and keeping things from me for most of my goddamn life! I tried to ignore it, to hide my feelings, but inside everything just kept building up until one day all the anger in me suddenly exploded, and I felt like yelling and screaming and striking out, and from then on all I cared about was proving to the whole damn world that I'm just as good as any man . . . an' better than some!' Before either Drifter or Macahan could say anything, she walked off, soon swallowed up by the surrounding darkness.

''Be a sonofabitch,' Macahan said. 'Seems like you'n me, Quint, we got a couple of bobcats by the tail.'

22

The two men had hobbled the horses, built a fire and were dunking hardtack biscuits in their coffee by the time the women returned to camp. Neither said a word — not about why they'd been gone so long, or what they had talked about or even why the men had eaten supper without them.

Nada.

Both merely filled their coffee mugs from the blackened pot sitting on the embers, took some hardtack and venison jerky from their saddle-bags, sat beside the fire and started working their molars.

Which suited Drifter and Macahan just fine. Shooting it out with a gun-fighter, bracing Stadtlander, or staring down an angry mob was one thing; dealing with two riled-up women was another. And neither man was even remotely interested in venturing into such hostile territory.

Finally, Liberty broke the silence. 'I been thinking,' she said to Macahan. ''Cept for Latigo, who's most likely gone to ground, nobody knows me around here. How 'bout first light I ride into town and get a smell of the land?'

'An' then what?'

'Report back to you — what else?'

Macahan considered her proposal and, to his credit, did not look at Drifter for his opinion. 'Could be dangerous.'

'So's drinking the water.'

'Couldn't hurt, I reckon.'

'That's what I figured,' Liberty said, pleased.

'We'll wait an hour. You ain't back by then, we'll be ridin' in.'

Liberty nodded. Rising, she finished her coffee, threw out the dregs, 'G'night one and all,' went to her horse, untied her bedroll and spread it on the ground near the fire.

Emily watched her. There was admiration and gratitude in her large, expressive brown eyes. 'Think I'll turn in, too,' she said, rising. She turned to Drifter, pecking him on the forehead. 'Good night, Father . . . Marshal . . . ' and walked to her horse.

'Sleep tight,' Drifter called after her. He sounded relieved. 'Reckon the war's over,' he said quietly to Macahan.

The tall, young, taciturn deputy US marshal nodded in agreement.

'Ain't no figurin' them, is there?'

'The trick,' Drifter said wisely, 'is not to even try.'

23

The coyotes were in full chorus when Liberty rode in the pre-dawn light toward Los Locos. There was a chilling bite to the air. Shivering, she pulled the collar of her duster up around her neck. Her breath clouded in front of her. But inside, where the truth lives, she could not have felt warmer. The years of being overlooked and ignored were behind her now, and ahead, if she did her job properly, lay a bright future as a lawman.

The word made her grimace. 'Law *man*!' she said, not realizing she'd thought aloud. 'How 'bout law *woman*? Is that so hard to say?' She laughed in disgust. Hell, would the world ever change and recognize women for their true worth? One day, maybe — though, truthfully, she doubted it. And sure as hens lay brown eggs, not in her lifetime.

In her mind she heard Marshal Thompson say in his deep, somber voice, 'Always remember: anythin' worth gittin' is worth waitin' for.'

So she'd waited, often with her teeth gritted, and after being passed over a half-dozen times and watching men inferior to her in all aspects of the job being sworn in as deputies, Marshal Thompson, a terse but fair-minded man who seldom strung more than three words together, gave her the news: he needed a deputy to replace Harv Wilbon, who was retiring — was she interested?

She had wanted to jumped up and hug him and scream YES! YES! as loudly as she could. But after years of disappointment, she knew better; restraining her excitement, she merely answered, 'Sure', and then went on filing away a pile of old wanted posters.

Marshal Thompson, after a curt nod, walked out of the office without another word, leaving Liberty to wonder if he had actually spoken to her or if she had imagined the whole thing.

She hadn't. A week later — two days after her thirty-fifth birthday — she was sworn in; the following day she had been sent into Indian Territory to arrest the oldest of the three McDermott brothers for knifing a whiskey drummer who had been 'sniffin'' around McDermott's dancehall wife longer than was deemed polite.

Now, as Liberty rode toward the outskirts of Los Locos, she thought about how easy that first arrest had been. The McDermotts lived in a sod-roofed shack in a box-canyon just across the line, and knowing that Indian Territory was out of the marshal's jurisdiction, had not been expecting a lawman to come after them. And when Liberty showed up, they had not taken her or her deputy US marshal's star seriously, instead believing it to be some kind of joke conjured up by friends or neighbors. As a result, the younger brothers, Charlie and Darryl, giggling like idiots, had actually fastened her handcuffs around the wrists of their brother, Lake, who, himself, happily played along with the joke until, too late, they all realized Liberty was not only serious but willing to back up the arrest with six-gun or shotgun, both of which, as the brothers stated later during the trial, 'she demonstrated a willingness to use'.

After that, and Lake's twenty-year sentence, word had quickly spread among the lawless element throughout Oklahoma and Indian Territory that Liberty, despite being a woman, was to be respected — even feared like any other deputy US marshal.

A dog barking interrupted Liberty's thoughts. She realized she was now riding into town, following a narrow dirt street that snaked between clusters of squat, ugly adobe dwellings that had been worn smooth by years of swirling desert winds and baked brown by incessant broiling sunlight.

Muted voices could be heard inside some of the hovels. Here and there a baby cried. And whenever she passed one of the many shuttered cantinas the smell of stale greasy cooking flooded her senses.

Ahead, the street ended at a small, silent, unlighted plaza. A gaunt yellow mutt suddenly ran, yapping, out of a side street, across in front of her. It startled both her and her horse, which crab-stepped so abruptly Liberty was almost thrown from the saddle. Reining up, she dropped her hand to her six-gun and gazed about her. A drunk was sleeping it off against a crumbling statue of the Madonna, his loud snoring disturbing the silence of the night. Other than that, the plaza was empty and graveyard-quiet.

Lantern light glimmered in the windows of two of the hovels facing the plaza, but the rest were dark. Liberty's wandering gaze passed over the rundown stores and cantinas encircling her and finally settled on the largest of the adobe dwellings. It was painted light blue with yellow ochre trim around the windows, had potted cacti outside the front door and was in better condition than the other buildings. There was nothing about the house that suggested danger, or even that it warranted a second look, but some inner instinct nagged at Liberty and, nudging her horse closer, she reined up outside the front door and listened intently. All was quiet inside. There was a pathetically thin, dead kitten lying in the dirt fronting the house, but no sign of hoofprints. Nor could she see El Diablo or any other horses tied up in the narrow dark alley that separated the house from the other dwellings.

Deciding to check behind the house, she rode down the alley and stopped when she came to a small fenced enclosure that she guessed was used as a corral. It was empty save for a milk goat tied to a post. Yet still the hair on her neck tingled — a sure sign that something was amiss. But what? Liberty sat there, astride the bay, listening, but again all was quiet. Deciding that her instincts were wrong, she was about to ride away, when she heard a faint metallic click behind her.

It was a familiar click, the deadly sound of a rifle being cocked, and an instant after hearing it Liberty threw herself from the saddle.

She was an instant too late. The rifle fired and a slug tore into her side, glanced off a rib and angled upward. The pain made her gasp. And even as she landed hard on the ground, winded but instinctively reaching for her Colt, Liberty knew she was badly hurt — perhaps done for.

It took all she had, but she managed to crawl across the alley and around behind the adjacent hovel. There, she sat with her back slumped against the wall, Colt clutched in her now useless right hand, staring numbly at the ever-growing bloodstain on her sun-faded denim shirt. She felt dizzy and, as she peered around the side of the house to see if anyone was coming, her vision became blurry. She blinked, hoping it would clear. It didn't. She leaned her

159

head back against the adobe wall and closed her eyes. Her life was draining away and she almost laughed at the absurdity of it: all those years of waiting to be accepted, to become a deputy US marshal, all her hopes and dreams, that bright future that had suddenly seemed within her grasp — all gone — and for what? To end up here — dying in an alley in a scummy Mexican pueblo filled with outlaws and border trash, worthless low-life of whom she had sworn to rid the world but who had in fact now gotten rid of her — seemed utterly senseless.

She didn't hear his footsteps approaching. But she did hear someone talking to her. And when she opened her eyes and looked up, through a hazy red blur she saw him standing over her, Winchester crooked in one arm, his boyishly handsome face twisted into a grimace, his free hand clutching at his ribs as if to ease the pain walking had caused.

His lips were moving but she couldn't make out what he was saying.

She stared at him, numbly, unable to move.

Finally his words reached her. 'Sorry it had to be you,' he said.

'D-Didn't give me a chance . . . '

'Couldn't take the risk.'

She guessed, in a muddled way, that was a compliment.

She worked her lips, but no sound came out.

'Where's Macahan an' the others?' he asked.

Again, she tried to speak and couldn't.

'How come they sent you in alone?'

Suddenly she felt very tired. Her eyelids became terrifically heavy. She fought to keep them open. But she couldn't and slowly they closed.

Then everything went deadly quiet. Still. Her life ended.

24

Dawn flooded the cloudy gray sky with daggers of lemon and lilac.

Over an hour had passed since Liberty had ridden off. Macahan, growing more and more concerned, decided to wait no longer. He gave the order to saddle up and the three of them rode in the direction of Los Locos.

They rode in silence. Each was busy with their own thoughts, their own reasons as to why Liberty hadn't returned. Drifter and Macahan's grim expressions revealed how they thought. Only Emily looked optimistic.

Soon they were within sight of the grubby little pueblo. They could see scattered lights in the outskirts. Here and there a cooking fire glowed. They rode closer. Macahan raised his hand, slowing their pace. He started to say something then stopped, abruptly, as a horse came trotting toward them.

It was a bay with a thin white blaze on its forehead and two white stockings and they realized, with sinking hearts, that the body draped across the saddle had to be Liberty.

Spurring their horses, they quickly reached the bay and closed in around it to prevent it from escaping. It snickered nervously, as if the corpse had made it skittish. Drifter leaned close and grabbed its trailing reins.

'Sonofa*bitch*,' Macahan said, dismounting and gently cupping his hands around Liberty's face. 'That no-good, hog-pukin' bastard!'

Drifter didn't say anything.

Emily started crying.

'I want it on record,' Macahan said. 'This is on me.'

'How you figure that?' Drifter asked.

'If she'd been a man, I never would've let him ride on in ahead.'

Emily angrily turned to him and through her tears, hissed: 'That's a hateful thing to say!'

'Didn't mean it like you think,' Macahan said.

'How then?' she demanded, disbelieving him.

'Meant, it's 'cause she was a woman an' I didn't want her to think I didn't trust her, didn't think she was up to it, that I agreed.' He paused, voice choked with uncharacteristic emotion, then added: 'Been a fella, I wouldn't have had them kind of notions. I would've acted like I should've, with reason and logic, and told him no . . . then he'd still be alive — she'd still be alive!' He turned his back on her and stared regretfully at the corpse, lips set in a tight grim line.

'Reckon you owe him an apology,' Drifter told his daughter.

Emily sniffed back her tears and apologized.

Macahan gave a curt nod and gently lifted the corpse off the horse. 'Get her bedroll for me,' he said to Drifter.

Drifter obeyed and helped him wrap Liberty in her blanket. 'You want to bury her here or later, back on US soil?'

'Later,' Macahan said. 'Fine woman like her, she don't deserve to be buried in a shit-hole like this.' He and Drifter placed the wrapped body over the saddle again and roped it down securely.

'I'll take care of her,' Emily said. 'If Latigo is holed up here, and is responsible for this — like I know you both think — you'll need your hands free for shooting.'

'You don't think he done this?' Drifter said.

'I didn't say that.'

'You reckon some horse-thief or gunman shot her?' Macahan said.

'Possible, isn't it? This hellhole's full of them, you said so yourself.'

'Possible, but not likely.'

'Why?'

' 'Cause I never knowed an outlaw yet who killed a lawman then was kindly enough to pick him up an' lay him across his own saddle. Mostly, they spit on the corpse, kick dirt in his face an' go buy drinks all around.'

Emily had no comeback. She desperately wanted to cry but wouldn't let herself, knowing that Liberty would not have approved — and, even in death, she so wanted her approval. She'd admired her so much . . . and was determined to emulate her. And now, just like that, Liberty was gone; and nothing anyone said could deaden the pain and dismay Emily felt over losing her, or the anger she felt for the man who'd shot her. All she could do was desperately hope it hadn't been Latigo.

'Here.' Drifter handed her the bay's reins. 'You ride behind us, all right?'

Emily nodded. Waiting until her father and Macahan were mounted and riding toward Los Locos, she fell in behind them.

25

On reaching the outskirts, Macahan saw
how narrow the dirt streets were and
signaled for them to ride in single file.
He then led them between some ram-
shackle buildings, past an old crumbling
wall that had once enclosed a Spanish
don's ranchero, unaware that this was
the same street Liberty had used an
hour or so earlier.

But in that hour the town had slowly
woken up. Dogs now wandered the streets,
nosing through garbage and urinating
on walls. Roosters crowed. White-clad
Mexican *campesinos*, their faces almost
hidden beneath wide-brimmed, high-
crowned sombreros, stood talking and
smoking in groups in the plaza. Barefoot women in bright-colored dresses
carried earthen pots on their heads to
the community well outside town. Dirty,
half-naked children chased each other

through the streets. But there was no sign of any *gringos*. *Gringos*, as every local knew, slept later than the whores they'd bedded the night before.

Macahan, Drifter and Emily now reached the last cross-street before entering the plaza.

'Hold it, Ezra,' Drifter said, reining up. 'If Juanita *is* hidin' Latigo, they'll see us once we ride into the plaza. Her house faces it.'

Macahan stopped his horse and looked back at Drifter. 'Any ideas?'

'If we cut down here,' Drifter said, indicating the cross-street, 'it leads to an alley that runs between the rear of the house and an old corral where customers leave their horses. We don't run into nobody, we ought to be able to get real close to the place without bein' seen.'

'How 'bout dogs? If they start barkin' — '

'Juanita hates dogs. Her house is full of scrawny orphan cats that keep spewin' out kittens for her kids to torment. Want me to lead the way?' he added.

Macahan shook his head. 'If anybody's goin' to get shot,' he said quietly, 'this time it'll be me.'

He nudged his horse forward.

Drifter and Emily followed. The cross-street was wide enough for two riders. Emily brought her buckskin alongside her father and gave him a sour look.

'Seems you know your way around here very well, Daddy.'

'Should.'

'Why? Were you a' — she searched for the word — 'customer of this Juanita woman?'

'Me'n an' half of Chihuahua. That surprise you?'

'Shouldn't it?'

He saw her eyes blaze, her mouth harden angrily.

'Maybe it's hard for you to understand, Daughter, but breakin' broomtails for wages ain't a shortcut to settlin' down. A man gets needy driftin' from ranch to ranch, town to town. He needs comfortin' an' most times he ain't too particular where he gets it or who he gets it from.'

'And of course, you told Momma about this *comforting*?'

'I didn't have to,' Drifter said, annoyed by her sarcasm. 'She was woman enough to realize it — which obviously you aren't.' He tapped his horse with his spurs. The cantankerous sorrel gave a little buck and then surged ahead of Emily's horse.

Shortly they reached the end of the cross-street. In front of them was another dirt street and across, as Drifter had described, was an alley leading between a double row of rundown adobe houses. Several raggedy children were playing in the alley, kicking around a ball made out of tightly wrapped cloth strips. They stopped as Macahan, Drifter and Emily approached and seeing they were *gringos*, ran up to and alongside them, hands upheld, begging for *pesos*.

Macahan dug out some coins and showed them to the children. 'You want these?'

'*Sí, sí, sí,*' they all clamored.

'Then stay here an' don't tell nobody you saw us.' He tossed the coins in the air and rode on. Drifter and Emily, still leading Liberty's horse, avoided the scrambling urchins and followed the lawman.

It only took them a few minutes to reach Juanita's house. No noise came from it and the alley and corral were empty. Reining up beside the same wall where Liberty had died, Macahan and Drifter dismounted, grabbed their Winchesters and handed their reins to Emily.

'What am I supposed to do,' she said, nerves making her testy, 'wait here while you two shoot it out with whoever's in the house?'

''Bout covers it,' Macahan said.

'You might need another gun.'

'What we need,' Drifter said, 'is to know that no one's stole our horses.'

'And if you don't come back?'

'Then you're free to marry Latigo,' he said, turning away.

It was then she realized how much she'd hurt him. 'Daddy — '

He turned back to her. 'Yeah?'

'What I said about comforting and Momma — that was spiteful and insensitive and I'm sorry. I truly am.'

Drifter studied her for a moment, anger melting. Then he returned beside her, pressed his hand over hers and squeezed fondly. 'No matter what I did,' he said, 'I never done it to hurt her.'

'I know.'

'An' I never quit lovin' her.'

'Momma knew that,' Emily said. 'It's what held her together.'

Drifter nodded, as if satisfied, then turned and rejoined Macahan. The two men moved quietly to the back door. A mewing at their feet caused them to look down. A half-starved cat with two hungry kittens had joined them, anxious to get into the house. Macahan rolled his eyes, pushed the animals aside with his boot and reached for the door handle. Immediately the cat ran between his feet, followed by its kittens. Their loud mewing and the noise of the cat frantically clawing at the door alarmed Drifter and he motioned to Macahan to let them in.

Exasperated, the lawman stepped back and opened the door.

Cat and kittens scrambled inside and disappeared into the darkness.

Instantly, someone in the house fired a shotgun.

The deafening blast lit up the darkness.

Double-nought buckshot blew the door off its hinges.

Broken chunks of it flew past Macahan and Drifter.

Flattened against the wall, they realized that but for the cats they would have been in the line of fire and killed. They stood there a moment and exchanged grateful looks. Then, without exposing themselves to the shooter, they aimed their Winchesters into the doorway and blasted away.

No return fire came from within the house.

'Reloadin',' Drifter said to Macahan.

The lawman kept firing until he, too, was empty. 'Reloadin'.'

A noisy silence followed.

Drifter levered in a round but before he could start firing, Latigo called out from in the house.

'Either you boys hit?'

'Nope.'

'Goddamn cats.'

'You?'

'Uh-uh. But next time, reckon I'll know better'n to fire a scattergun with broken ribs.'

'There ain't goin' to be no next time,' Macahan said grimly. 'This ends right here an' now.'

'You in that much of a rush to die?'

'No more'n Liberty was,' Drifter said.

'Ahh . . . You found her, huh?'

'Wasn't that your intention?'

Silence.

'So it *was* you who killed her?' Macahan said.

'What did you expect? Hell, you sent her in.'

'An' it'll chew on me till the day I die.'

'Not me,' Latigo said. 'Way I figure, she give up bein' a woman once she pinned on that star.'

'A bullet in the ribs,' Drifter said. 'You didn't give her much of a chance.'

'I give her exactly the same chance you'd give me.'

Macahan spat disgustedly. 'You want a chance, throw down your guns an' come out, hands high.'

'Then what — a long ride to a hangin'?'

'Man makes his own future,' Macahan said.

'Man makes his own choices,' Latigo corrected. 'His future's decided for him — an' it always ends feet up.'

'Yeah, but it's the ride gettin' there that counts,' Drifter said. 'An' right now you're ridin' a blind mule over a cliff.'

Silence — save for a painful grunt from Latigo.

'What's it goin' to be?' Macahan said.

Long silence.

Then two ivory-grip, nickel-plated Colt .44s came bouncing out through the doorway. Drifter picked one up, examined it and nodded to Macahan.

'It's Shorty's.'

'You sound surprised.'

'Ain't like him to give up this easy.'

'Must be hurt more'n he's lettin' on.'

'Must be.'

'You in there alone?' Macahan called out.

'Just me'n the goddamn cats.'

'OK,' Macahan said, 'then come on out.'

'I'm tryin' to, dammit . . . ' Inside, there was the sound of someone struggling to get up, grunts of pain, followed by the same someone slowly, painfully, hobbling toward the door.

Finally, Latigo appeared, one hand held above his head, the other clutching his broken ribs. His face was etched with agony.

'Goddamn shotgun,' he said through clenched teeth. 'Kick damn near done me in.'

He got no sympathy from Macahan. 'Search him,' he told Drifter.

Drifter obeyed. 'Clean,' he said after patting Latigo down. 'Where's Juanita?'

'Bitch took off on me when she heard I'd shot a lawman. Stole El Diablo while she was at it, damn her eyes!' He heard a horse snicker and turned toward the alley where Emily stood holding the three horses. For an instant his heart jumped; then controlling his emotions, he said, 'Never figured I'd see you again.'

'I had to find out for myself,' Emily said, tears glinting in her eyes.

'Find out what?'

'If you really are the heartless killer everyone claimed you were.'

'Reckon you got your answer,' Latigo said, indicating Liberty's blanket-covered corpse.

Emily swallowed hard before answering. 'Yes, I have,' she said bitterly, 'and in the process, lost a wonderful friend.'

'Everything's got a price,' Latigo said. He seemed to be taunting her yet he was unable to hide the genuine sadness and regret in his amber-colored eyes. 'Even friendship.'

'Thanks to you,' Emily said, 'I'm beginning to learn that.'

For several moments they continued to look at each other. Then, as if bothered by the burning disappointment clouding her eyes, Latigo turned to Macahan and offered out his wrists. 'C'mon, Marshal,' he said brusquely. 'Let's get this over with.'

26

The four of them rode slowly, warily through town.

Emily now rode double behind her father, one hand clasped around his waist, the other gripping the reins of Liberty's bay. Macahan and Latigo rode, side-by-side, ahead of them. The big, tight-lipped lawman kept his hand on the butt of his six-gun, ready to draw and shoot anyone who tried to stop them — or Latigo if he tried to escape.

But the little Texan appeared to be in too much pain to try anything. Sitting astride Emily's buckskin, hands cuffed in front of him, he grunted and winced with every step the horse made.

As they followed the same narrow dirt street by which they'd entered town, Macahan and Drifter kept a sharp eye out for trouble. There was none. It was still barely daylight, too early for any of the gunmen and border trash to have dragged themselves out of bed and the local Mexicans, many of them simple *campesinos*, were only too happy to see these troublesome *gringos* leave.

At last they reached the outskirts. Ahead, the street ran between a row of dilapidated dwellings and the ancient crumbling ranchero wall before spilling out into the desert. As they approached the end of the wall, the rising sun cleared the distant mountains to the east. It was now in their eyes, forcing Drifter and Macahan to pull their hats down lower.

As they did, Latigo cruelly dug his spurs into the buckskin's flanks and jerked back on the reins, causing the startled horse to whinny and rear up, forelegs pawing at the air.

Its actions frightened the other horses. Macahan's gray lunged sideways to avoid the flailing hoofs while, behind, Drifter's sorrel, Wilson, added to the chaos by biting the gray on the rump. It screamed and bucked, almost throwing Macahan, who fought to get the angry horse under control.

Drifter, with Emily clinging on behind him, did the same with his sorrel. It wasn't easy. The irascible horse, always eager to bite him, swung its head around and tried to grab his boot. Cursing, Drifter jerked his foot from the stirrup and clamping down on the reins, gradually managed to subdue the sorrel.

By then, Latigo had kicked his horse and ridden away from them.

But he did not ride far. Instead, he stopped as he reached the end of the street, turned his horse around and faced Macahan, Drifter and Emily.

For a moment it appeared as if he were daring Macahan and Drifter to shoot him.

But then, before they had time to draw their Colts, a string of riders trotted out from behind the old wall and lined up beside him. There were twenty of them. All had drooping black mustaches, wore high-crowned sombreros and bandoleers slung over their shoulders, were heavily armed, and, by their fierce-eyed expressions, eager to start shooting.

'Meet my friends,' Latigo said. He indicated the *bandidos*, the gesture making him grimace with pain. 'They're a mite rough around the edges, as you'd say, Emily, but what they lack in manners, they more'n make up for in loyalty an' their hatred of *gringos*.'

As if to confirm their hatred the bandits angrily brandished their rifles and shouted: '*Muerte a los gringos! Muerte a los gringos!*'

'I'm impressed,' said Drifter, sounding anything but. 'Figurin' on startin' your own revolution, are you?'

Latigo started to laugh — then stopped as pain shot through his ribs.

'I wonder how they'd feel about you,' Emily said, disgustedly, 'if they knew you'd been paid to murder Mexican ranchers so a rich greedy *gringo* cattleman could steal their land?'

Latigo lost his smile. But before he could reply, the bandit leader, Chico Perez, rode out from behind the wall . . . followed by Juanita, a sombrero hanging down her back, her long black hair wild and loose about her bare shoulders, astride a magnificent blue roan stallion that brought a faint gasp from Emily.

'El Diablo!' she exclaimed. 'What's she doing with my horse?'

'Reckon he give it to her,' put in Drifter, 'as payment for lettin' him hole up here.'

'You b-bastard!' Emily began.

Perez stopped her by shooting his gaudy, silver-plated pistol in the air. '*Silencio!*' he bellowed. '*No es el lugar para habla aqui!*'

'I'll speak when I want to,' Emily said defiantly. 'That's my horse! And he' — she pointed at Latigo — 'stole it from me and — '

Again Perez fired his silver-plated pistol into the air. A big man of fifty, with a double-chin and a bulging belly beneath his blue, gold-braided Mexican general's tunic, he had the insincere smile of a dictator. 'Speak again, *señorita*,' he told Emily, 'and I will shoot you. *Comprende?*'

'Don't prod him,' Latigo warned. 'Not if you want to see tomorrow.'

Emily grudgingly subsided.

Perez turned to Latigo. 'Why do you wait, *señor*? My men, they are anxious to kill all these *Yanqui* pigs.'

'Patience, *amigo*,' Latigo said. 'You'll get your wish — soon as I'm done talkin' to the marshal.' To Macahan, he added, 'You interested in a trade?'

'What sort of trade?' Macahan said.

'Me for Emily.'

'No!' she blurted. 'Don't do it, Ezra! Don't agree to anything he says.'

'Done,' Macahan said, adding: 'But her pa an' me have to be there, at the border, to make sure she gets safely into the States, otherwise no deal.'

'No-o,' begged Emily. Then to Drifter, 'I won't do it, Daddy. I won't go if you and Ezra don't come with me.'

'Sorry,' Latigo said before Drifter could answer. 'That ain't on the cards. I'm not spendin' the rest of my days lookin' over my shoulder for Macahan — or your pa, for that matter. Now,' he added to both men, 'we got a trade or not?'

'Sure,' Drifter said. 'But like Macahan says: only if we watch Emily cross the line.'

'You are a fool,' Perez said to Latigo. 'Why waste time talking about trades? I say shoot them all now and let us be done with it!'

'No,' Juanita said. 'There will be no more killing of women. That is final!'

The bandit leader sucked in his belly and postured indignantly. '*No me diga que hacer, mujer!*'

Juanita laughed scornfully. 'You did not mind me telling you what to do in my brass bed, *Gordo!*'

The bandit leader cringed and, losing his bluster, tried to save face before his men: '*Lo hare por ti, mi amor.* But in return for my favor you will give me your horse.'

Juanita turned to Latigo. 'I must have something for my trouble.'

Latigo shrugged, and said to Drifter, 'You know how mercenary she is. You want to save Emily, one of you better ante up some money. *Pronto.*'

'What I got wouldn't save a three-legged coyote,' Macahan said.

Drifter's silence suggested his pockets were empty too.

'I have money,' Emily blurted. 'Twenty-dollar gold pieces! Lots of them — in my saddle-bags. Remember,' she said to Latigo, 'I told you about how Pa Mercer used to give me money every time he came to see me at St Mark's? I still have most of it.'

Latigo nodded. 'Yeah, I remember.' He turned to Juanita. 'She's got about two hundred in gold. Interested?'

'*Sí.*' Juanita climbed down from her saddle and handed El Diablo's reins to the bandit leader. 'Here, Chico. Now, give me your horse.'

As Perez dismounted and ran his hands admiringly over the stallion,

Emily slid down from behind Drifter and hurried over to the bay carrying Liberty's blanket-wrapped corpse.

Puzzled, Drifter watched as his daughter unfastened the strap that kept the flap closed and reached inside the leather bag.

A moment later Emily pulled out a cloth-wrapped object. 'If you don't mind,' she said, as she unfolded the cloth, 'I'd like to keep the box. It belonged to my mother and — ' She stopped, dropped the cloth revealing a Colt .45 — Liberty's Colt .45 — and barely taking aim, shot the bandit leader in the leg.

He collapsed with a scream and lay writhing on the ground.

Emily ran over to him and pressed the Colt against his head.

'Tell your men to drop their weapons,' she ordered, 'or I swear I will kill you.'

Chico Perez saw the calm, quiet rage in Emily's brown eyes and knew she meant it.

'*Hombres, dejen caer su armas.*'

'Hurry,' Emily said as the bandits reluctantly obeyed their leader. 'Guns, knives, everything. *Pronto, hombres!*' To emphasize her words, she pressed the Colt even harder against Perez's head and thumbed back the hammer.

Drifter and Macahan, meanwhile, quickly dismounted and drawing their six-guns, covered Latigo and the *bandidos.* When they were all disarmed, Emily stepped back and beckoned to Juanita, who grudgingly joined her. 'We're taking him with us,' she said, referring to Perez. 'Find something to bandage him up with, so he doesn't bleed to death on the way.'

Juanita studied her, half-admiringly, half-amused. 'You are very young, *señorita.* How did you learn to be so brave?'

'I had a good teacher,' Emily said. Her gaze wandered from Drifter to Liberty's corpse. 'Two good teachers.'

27

When Perez was ready to travel, Macahan ordered one of the bandits to give up his horse and to help his leader onto the saddle. 'The rest of you stay here,' he added to the other men. 'Once we're safely across the border, we'll let him go.'

'How do we know you speak the truth?' another bandit demanded. 'For all we know, you might intend to kill him.' Immediately the other *bandidos* joined in, agreeing with him, some of them pressing forward menacingly.

Macahan, Drifter and Emily fired at their feet, driving them back.

'*Alto! Alto!*' Juanita waved the angry bandits back. 'Do not worry about Chico,' she assured them. 'I will go with the *gringos* to make sure they keep their word.'

'Do as she says,' Perez said as his

189

men hesitated. 'Return to the plaza and wait for me there. *Consiga que va, muchachos!*'

Grudgingly, the bandits mounted up, whirled their horses around and rode back into town.

Macahan watched them for a few moments to make sure they didn't turn back, then climbed into the saddle and rode up alongside Latigo. 'I ain't never killed an unarmed man, or a prisoner,' he said softly, 'but if you so much as twitch wrong 'tween here an' the line, I'll happily make an exception. We clear on that, bounty hunter?'

'Real clear,' Latigo said — and, for once, said no more.

Macahan looked back at Drifter, who, Winchester resting across his saddle, was mounted alongside Perez and Juanita. Drifter nodded at the lawman to show he was ready.

Satisfied, Macahan turned to Emily, who, now astride El Diablo, was still holding the reins of the bay. 'I never got to know Liberty much,' he said, his tone respectful, 'but one thing I can pretty much guarantee, Miss Emily, she'd be right proud to know you were bringin' her home.'

With that, he faced front, nudged his horse forward and led the little party out into the hot open scrubland.

* * *

It was mid-morning when the four of them crossed the border. Reining up beside Eagle Rock, they looked back at Juanita and Chico Perez, who were still on Mexican soil.

'You're free to go now,' Macahan told them.

The bandit leader, weak from loss of blood but still defiant, angrily spat on the ground. 'You have won this time, *gringos*. But we Mexicans, we are a patient people. I will wait. And next time you come to Chihuahua, it will reach my ears and I promise you, you will never leave again.'

Drifter, unimpressed, tipped his hat

to Juanita. 'Take good care of them cats o' yours,' he said. 'I got a warm fuzzy spot in my heart for them.'

Juanita frowned, puzzled. 'I do not understand, *hombre*. Always before, you hate my cats.'

'Man's entitled to change his mind, ain't he?' Drifter said. 'Hell, women do it all the time.' He looked at Emily and gave her a fatherly wink.

She smiled, thinking how at that moment she loved him more than anything.

★   ★   ★

It was a small, quiet, private funeral.

The gravesite was atop a low grassy rise at the west end of the drab Santa Rosa cemetery and though the morning was cool and cloudy, the sun came out to witness the brief service.

Drifter, Emily, Macahan, Father Guiterrez and two old Mexican gravediggers were the only people who attended. That had been Emily's idea.

It was how Liberty would have wanted it, she said. No frills. Just the respect and acknowledgement of those who came after her that she had been an integral part of the office she'd sworn to serve — and in doing so, had in a tiny way, along with the other two female deputy US marshals, helped make it easier for any women in the future who wanted to become officers of the law.

Macahan, who still blamed himself for Liberty's death, insisted that the marshals' office pay for everything, including the coffin, a wreath and a stone marker bearing her name and, below, the date she died.

There was no kin to notify. No one even knew the date she was born. Not even Marshal Thompson in Guthrie, whose quick reply to Macahan's overnight wire was typically terse but meaningful.

SHE WILL BE SORELY MISSED STOP HER LOYALTY AND DEDICATION TO DUTY UNMATCHED STOP HER

LOSS IS THE GOOD LORD'S GAIN
US MARSHAL THOMPSON

His cryptic message seemed to sum up Liberty perfectly. And in the telegraph office when Macahan had showed the wire to Drifter and Emily, Emily had read it carefully, closed her eyes and then read it again, and then, biting back tears, asked the lawman if she could keep it.

'Wish I could oblige,' he said somberly, 'but I need it for my report.' Then, as she looked disappointed, ''Course, I been known to lose things now and then an' if this here wire was to fall out of my pocket, say, an' someone happened to pick it up an' not tell me, well, then, reckon I'd just have to tell the marshal I lost it.' Taking the wire from her, he tucked it in the pocket of his sun-faded denim jacket in such a careless way that as soon as he started for the door the wire dropped to the floor. Without looking back he walked out, Drifter on his heels, leaving

Emily alone. Grateful, she picked up the wire, folded it carefully and tucked it into her pocket.

Now, with the funeral over, Emily looked at the wire one more time. It tied a knot in her throat. But she somehow fought down her emotions and promised herself — and Liberty — that she would not cry again. She then followed her father and Macahan down the slope to the gate. There, just outside, stood a horse-drawn tarp-covered wagon that earlier they had rented from Lars Gustafson to carry the coffin, and that had remained unattended but clearly visible to Macahan during the service. Though it appeared empty once the coffin had been removed, now, as Macahan rolled back one end of the tarp, a man in leg-irons and handcuffs peered up at them.

'Fella could suffocate in here,' Latigo grumbled, as Drifter helped him sit up and handed him a canteen.

'Don't give me ideas,' Macahan growled.

'Wouldn't take much right now for me to tie a sack over your goddamn head an' save the marshals' office a one-way ticket to El Paso.' He stomped off.

Latigo took a gulp of the warm, metallic-tasting water and then splashed some over his head. 'Our marshal, he ain't a man who forgives easy, is he?'

'Can you blame him?' Drifter said. 'You're stuck in his craw like a piece of gristle that no amount of swallowin' can ever wash down — not even if the law decides to hang you.'

'Maybe he should've thought of that,' Latigo said, ' 'fore he sent a woman to do his job for him.'

Emily, who'd been standing behind her father, now angrily pushed him aside and glared at Latigo.

'I once thought I loved you,' she said bitterly. 'I don't know how or why, but I did. I would have willingly gone with you anywhere, even though it was against my father's wishes — '

Latigo cut her off. 'If you got somethin' to say, girl, spit it out.'

'What I have to say is this,' Emily said. 'If you soil Liberty's name one more time between now and when you and the marshal board the train, you won't have to worry about hanging 'cause I will shoot you myself.' She stormed off.

Latigo looked after her for a moment then turned back to Drifter.

'Damn,' he said, 'I sure pity the poor sonofabitch who ends up with that little gal.'

'Pity or envy?'

'What're you talkin' about?'

'Just 'tween us, OK?'

'Just 'tween us, what?'

Drifter studied him intently. 'I'm curious.'

''Bout?'

'Why a man who claims to have no conscience would deliberately drive away the gal he cared about. Why is that, d'you think?'

The little Texan chuckled. 'You got that ass-backwards, *amigo*. Emily cut me loose, not the other way 'round.'

'Nice try, Shorty, but no cigar. Emily

told me everything that was said 'tween you'n her at the jail. An' though she can't see it, to me, knowin' you long as I have an' rememberin' what it takes to knot your tail, it's as clear as sippin' whiskey . . . '

'If'n it's that clear,' Latigo said, 'how come I don't know what the hell you're runnin' your mouth about?'

'Then let me spell it out for you: despite all your denials an' attempts to hide it, deep down you got a conscience like everybody else — '

'Like hell — '

' — an' 'cause of that conscience,' Drifter continued, 'you had a moment of guilt.'

'You're loco to the bone, you know that?'

Drifter chuckled. 'Don't sweat it,' he said. 'I ain't aimin' to tell anyone — least of all Emily. But it just goes to show how savvy my little gal is.'

'Meanin'?'

'She had you pegged all along. Said, no matter how evil folks thought you were, or how mean an' unforgiving bad you were, deep down, where no one lies, not even to themselves, you were a decent man.' He turned and started away then stopped, looked back at the little gun-fighter, said, 'An' for that, Shorty, I'll always thank you.'

'Like I said,' Latigo called after him. 'Loco to the bone.'

28

They arrived at the train station shortly after sunset. Leaving her father and Macahan guarding the tarp-covered wagon, Emily dismounted and entered the stationhouse — almost bumping into the old, spindly stationmaster, Mr Cripps, who was locking up.

'Ooops, sorry, sorry, Miss Emily,' he clucked. 'But I'm late for supper and — '

'It's all right, Mr Cripps. You go ahead. I'll buy the tickets on the train.'

'Yes, yes, that's fine,' he said, adding, 'It's on time so you shouldn't have long to wait. Good night, good night.'

'G'night, Mr Cripps.' Emily watched as he hurried off toward town. She then went around to the tiny plank-platform and made sure no one was waiting there. Satisfied that she was alone, she walked to the corner of the stationhouse and signaled to Macahan to come ahead.

The lawman rolled back the tarp and, with Drifter's help, got Latigo out of the wagon. The little bounty hunter was still cuffed and in leg-irons and moved stiffly. He grunted painfully as he hobbled along between them but did not say a word.

Once on the platform, Macahan remained beside Latigo, rifle crooked over his arm, eyes sweeping the open scrubland for any sign of Stadtlander and his men.

At the same time Drifter and Emily went to the east and west corners of the stationhouse and looked toward town for the same reason.

Ten tense minutes dragged by.

Dusk settled around them. Insects whined about their ears.

Then a distant whistle told them the train was coming.

Latigo spoke for the first time since getting out of the wagon. 'I got somethin' to say to Emily,' he told Macahan.

The lawman, about to deny the

request, reconsidered. 'Emily,' he called out, 'you interested in hearin' anythin' this man's got to say?'

She started to say no; then she too reconsidered and joined them.

'Yes?'

'Alone,' Latigo said to Macahan.

The tall, big-shouldered lawman grudgingly stepped aside, but continued to watch Latigo, ready for any sudden moves.

'Go ahead,' Emily said coldly. 'I'm listening.'

Latigo chewed on his thoughts for a moment before saying: 'I been on this earth almost forty years an' in all that time I ain't never said sorry to no one.'

'I don't think that's anything to be proud of,' Emily said.

If he heard her, he showed no sign of it.

In fact he was silent so long, she said: 'Is that it — what you wanted to tell me?'

'Reckon so.'

Emily sighed, disappointed for some reason, and walked back to her position.

* * *

Two passengers got off the train. Neither Drifter nor Emily knew them, but they remained alongside Macahan and Latigo — just in case.

But after giving the prisoner quick, curious looks, both men hurried on into town.

Drifter and Emily remained on the platform, watching as Macahan helped Latigo board the train and then shuffle on into the first passenger car.

There were two empty window seats facing each other. Latigo took one, Macahan the other. The young lawman then lowered the window and poked his head out.

'Reckon you know how much I'm obliged to you,' he said to Drifter and Emily, adding, 'If you're ever in El Paso, be sure to stop by the marshals' office an' look me up.'

'I hope you mean that,' Emily said, 'because soon as I turn eighteen I intend to.'

Surprised, Drifter looked at Macahan and shrugged. 'News to me,' he said.

Emily said, 'According to Liberty, I'll be old enough then to work in the marshals' office . . . and maybe one day become a deputy.'

Macahan put it together then and smiled. 'When that day comes,' he assured her, 'call on me. I'll do all I can to help.'

The locomotive blew its shrill whistle, steam hissed, and a moment later the train lurched into motion.

Drifter and Emily waved goodbye and Macahan started to raise the window.

Latigo suddenly pushed him aside and, ignoring the pain knifing through his ribs, stuck out his head and looked back at Emily.

Her back was turned to him as she and Drifter walked toward their horses.

'Sorry,' Latigo said softly.

Emily could not have possibly heard

him above the noise of the train pulling away. But as if drawn by some inner feeling, she glanced back and saw Latigo leaning out of the window.

She wasn't sure but she thought she saw his lips move.

Then he was jerked back inside by an angry Macahan, who pushed Latigo down in his seat and raised the window.

Wondering what it was that Latigo had said, she shrugged it off and continued walking beside her father.

* * *

When they reached their horses, Drifter grasped her by the arm and turned her toward him.

'Becomin' a deputy marshal,' he said quietly, 'you mean that?'

She nodded. 'Guess I should've told you first, but . . . '

'Seems I remember you mentionin' it once.'

Silence save for insects whining about their ears. Then, 'You think it's possible, Daddy? I mean, could I actually become a deputy US marshal?'

Drifter chuckled and gently fisted her on the chin. 'You, my daughter, can do anythin' you put your mind to. Proved that a long time ago.'

'Yes,' she said determinedly. 'You're right. I can. Bet I'd be a good deputy, too.'

She reached up on tiptoe and kissed his weathered, stubbly cheek.

'*Tequiro mucho, papa.*'

'Love you too,' he said.

They untied their horses, Drifter automatically avoiding the quick little nip from the sorrel, and mounted up.

'Oh, one other thing,' Emily said, as they rode slowly into town. 'I plan on changing my first name.'

'What to,' he said, no longer surprised by anything she said. 'President of the United States?'

'Silly. That's a title.'

'Well, shame on me.'

'To Liberty.'

'Liberty?' He was wrong, he realized.

He could still be surprised. 'Why Liberty?'

''Cause she's my hero. And since she was an orphan, I'm the only one who can keep her name alive.'

Drifter didn't say anything.

'You aren't angry, are you?'

'Not angry, no.'

'What, then?'

'Disappointed.'

'Disappointed? Why?'

'I kind of hoped I was your hero.'

'You,' Emily said fondly, 'are my father. That's way more important than any hero.'

Drifter grunted, as if appeased. He'd only been joking anyway, but he was still glad to hear her say it.

THE END

We do hope that you have enjoyed reading this large print book.

Did you know that all of our titles are available for purchase?

We publish a wide range of high quality large print books including:
Romances, Mysteries, Classics
General Fiction
Non Fiction and Westerns

Special interest titles available in large print are:
The Little Oxford Dictionary
Music Book, Song Book
Hymn Book, Service Book

Also available from us courtesy of Oxford University Press:
Young Readers' Dictionary
(large print edition)
Young Readers' Thesaurus
(large print edition)

For further information or a free brochure, please contact us at:
Ulverscroft Large Print Books Ltd.,
The Green, Bradgate Road, Anstey,
Leicester, LE7 7FU, England.
Tel: (00 44) 0116 236 4325
Fax: (00 44) 0116 234 0205